I0741616

Best of Books By the Bed #2

What Writers Are Reading Before Lights Out

Edited by Cheryl Olsen and Eric Olsen

BRIGHTCITYBOOKS
brightcitybooks.com

ISBN: 978-0-9795898-8-1

Edited by Cheryl Olsen and Eric Olsen
Cover photo and cover design by Bill Girsch
Painting in cover photo, *G$-DR-01*, by David Ryan

Thanks!

We are enormously indebted to the generosity of the contributors herein, as well as to writers everywhere whose love of language and words and their purposeful arrangement on the page enrich all our lives.

Books and their methods of dissemination may change, but readers will continue to seek them out, to plumb their depths, and to share their myriad contents. And that, friends, is what this book is all about.

CONTENTS

Introduction

This new edition of *Best of Books by the Bed* includes the contributions of 28 writers, "snapshots" of what they were reading at the time they first posted on our website, wewantedtobewriters.com, plus books by the bed that they intended to read next, and books they had read but hadn't yet put away. These give us a look at a special sort of reading, or as contributor Lee Upton puts it:

> I am a susceptible reader right before bed, when I feel most porous and undefended. And so the books by my bed have, for the most part, a peculiar quality—they tend to be more otherworldly and dreamlike than other books I enjoy, and less often marked by overt or unrelenting violence or violence that isn't somehow mediated.

This collection's co-editor, Eric Olsen, was particularly struck by Upton's aversion to books with violence, since he quite enjoys a nice murder mystery of an evening, whether marked by overt or unrelenting violence, or not.... (He's presently re-reading, for the umpteenth time, *Gorky Park* by Martin Cruz Smith, which of course famously opens with three "poor dead bastards." Has anyone ever written a more engaging opening? Eric's always hoping something of *Gorky Park* will rub off.)

Upton was not the only one to express preferences for certain types of reading late at night. "I try to fall asleep with good sentences in my ears," writes Dani Shapiro.

"I'm just starting to write a new book," says Miranda Beverly-Whittemore, "which means I have to be careful about the language and ideas coming in, because I'm easily swayable (it can throw me off course to digest something at the wrong moment of book gestation)."

Kathie Giorgio likes to read poetry before she falls asleep. "Poetry before bed feels right to me," she writes. "It can adjust itself to my level of sleepiness. Poetry is like the reverse of a snooze alarm. I can slap a page and get just a bit more, and then roll over to go to sleep, happy, contented."

And Tom Titus writes about the books by his bed:

> They pile up…. from a distance I see that the volumes accumulating there do have some things in common. They are nearly all poetry, essay collections, and other nonfiction that can be read in the short space of consciousness preceding that dark inexorable wave that sweeps it all away.

This edition of selected posts from the titular blog series contains discussions of more 250 books, more fiction than nonfiction this time, compared with the first edition, and about the same amount of poetry. You'll see in the appendix, which includes the more than 60 books by our contributors, that we've organized the books they discuss by genre. We've also included the page numbers where each book is discussed, for your convenience.

As we assembled this collection, we found ourselves writing down "must reads." Cheryl's list includes a bushel of fiction by women, and Eric's? Close to 20 titles and counting so far, including, most certainly, *The Dead Beat: Lost Souls, Lucky Stiffs, and the Perverse Pleasures of Obituaries* by Marilyn Johnson, discussed by Kitty Sheehan (see page 66). Also now on his must-read list are several books discussed by David Corbett about the criminal mind, including *Meeting the Shadow: The Hidden Power of the Dark Side of Human Nature* (see page 16). What's not to like?

As you read through this edition of *Best of*, we wish you your own list of must reads. And of course we'd love to know what books are by your bed. Please drop by wewantedtobewriters.com/books-by-the-bed and add your list to the comment box.

The Editors

Larry Baker

Although he had been publishing short stories since he was a teenager, Larry was 50 before his first novel, *The Flamingo Rising*, was published in 1997. *Flamingo* was one of three finalists for the Barnes and Noble Great New Voices award for 1997, a *Los Angeles Times* Top 100 book for 1997, and chosen by the Iowa Center for the Book to represent Iowa at the 2010 National Book Festival in Washington. And it was adapted for a Hallmark TV movie. With those pro-family credentials established, *Flamingo* was also included on the American Library Association's Banned Books list for 2011 after it was removed from a summer reading list for high-school students in Illinois.

His third novel, *A Good Man* (2009), was nominated for Book of the Year by the Southeast Independent Booksellers Association in 2010. He was also included on the Iowa Literary Walk of Fame that same year, joining other writers such as John Irving, Marilynne Robinson, Kurt Vonnegut, and Flannery O'Connor.

His fourth novel, *Love and Other Delusions*, is a dramatic departure for Larry in style and theme—"definitely not Hallmark material."

Early buzz for his latest novel, *The Education of Nancy Adams*, was enough to get Larry selected as the "Writer on Tour" by the Florida Literary Arts Council. He will be hosted by numerous Florida colleges in the Fall of 2014 and Spring of 2015.

You can read an excerpt from Larry's latest at: wewantedtobewriters.com/2014/06/excerpt-from-larry-bakers-new-novel.

Richard Beeman, *Plain Honest Men* — I save a lot of books every year for my well-deserved beach vacation in St. Augustine, Florida. The first book I am reading this summer at the beach will be Beeman's history of the Constitutional Convention. Truth is, I am *re-reading* the Beeman book. I feel there is much I need to re-absorb. It is one of those books, I tell my students, that ought to be required reading for any politician who spouts off about the Founding Fathers and the sacred concept of Original Intent. Beeman brings alive every single day of the Convention, the personalities involved, the issues debated, the gossip, the drinking, the intrigue, and the entire messy business of creating a new government in the midst of social disintegration, a creation only made possible by compromises that galled those who finally agreed. The "truth" of American history is much more compelling than the mythology that is blathered on the campaign trail. Books like this make me a better history teacher. Books like this also make me a smarter voter.

Keith Donohue, *The Boy Who Drew Monsters* — As for fiction, this is the book I want to read this summer, but it won't be released until October. Donohue's first novel, *The Stolen Child*, is one of my all-time favorites. How much did I like it? I bought a dozen hardcover editions and gave them away as gifts. I've never done that for any other book. His new book sounds great: "Ever since he nearly drowned in the ocean three years earlier, ten-year-old Jack Peter Keenan has been deathly afraid to venture outdoors. Refusing to leave his home in a small coastal town in Maine, Jack Peter spends his time drawing monsters. When those drawings take on a life of their own, no one is safe from the terror they inspire."

Bob Inman, *The Governor's Lady* — As for books in hand, I'll reach first for this one. Already liking his *Dairy Queen Days* and *Captain Saturday* would be enough of an incentive, but the real interest came from my wife's enthusiasm about the book. How do I know she liked it? She gave me an update each time she finished reading a chapter or two. She *really* wanted to talk about the book, and that is always a good sign.

Lady is about Cooper Lanier, a woman governor of a southern state who is succeeding her husband: "On her first day, as the state is blindsided by a blizzard, Cooper quickly realizes she is surrounded by leftovers from her husband's administration and that he intends to manage the state's affairs from the campaign trail, even if it means undermining her every command. Cooper is faced with the stark choice of seizing control or becoming a phony, irrelevant figurehead." I love politics, and I love Inman's writing. *Govenor's Lady* should be a pleasure.

Martha Woodroof, *Small Blessings* — Choosing another beach book was made a lot easier after meeting Martha Woodroof at the Virginia Festival of the Book back in March. If her first novel is as entertaining as my conversation with her in Charlottesville, I'm in for a fun read. Consider this: "Tom Putnam has resigned himself to a quiet and half-fulfilled life. An English professor in a sleepy college town, he spends his days browsing the Shakespeare shelves at the campus bookstore, managing the oddball faculty in his department and caring, alongside his formidable mother-in-law, for his wife Marjory, a fragile shut-in with unrelenting neuroses, a condition exacerbated by her discovery of Tom's brief and misguided affair with a visiting poetess a decade earlier." A story with "unrelenting neuroses" and "misguided" affairs… what's not to like?

Jincy Willett, *Amy Falls Down* — I only have a week at the beach, and I am a slow reader, right? So my final selection has to be a sure thing. Enter Jincy Willett. I am a big fan of her 2003 novel *Winner of the National Book Award*, and I have delayed reading *Amy Falls Down* for too long. Willett is a wry writer and *Amy* might be a perfect book for a "mature" reader such as myself: "Amy Gallup is an aging novelist and writing instructor living in Escondido, California, with her dog, Alphonse. Since recent unsettling events, she has made some progress. While she still has writer's block, she doesn't suffer from it. She's still a hermit, but she has allowed some of her class members into her life. She is no longer numb, angry, and sardonic: she is merely numb and bemused, which is as close to happy as she plans to get." And, yes, the plot involves her literally falling down. So, a story about an old writer who falls down a lot…I should have written this book.

All in all, August in Florida, under a tent on the beach, listening to the Atlantic, with a stack of good books. To steal a thought from Martha Woodroof, my life is a series of small blessings.

Posted June 6, 2014.

Nichole Bernier

Nichole Bernier is author of the novel *The Unfinished Work of Elizabeth D.*, which spent eight weeks on the *Boston Globe* Bestseller List and was a finalist for the 2012 New England Independent Booksellers Association fiction award. She has written for publications including *Psychology Today*, *Elle*, *Health*, *Salon*, *The Millions*, and *Post Road Literary Magazine*. A Contributing Editor for *Conde Nast Traveler* for 14 years, she was previously on staff as the magazine's golf and ski editor, columnist, and television spokesperson. She received her MS from the Columbia Graduate School of Journalism and is a founder of the literary blog *Beyond the Margins,* and lives outside of Boston with her husband and five children.

Visit her at her website, nicholebernier.com/, or on twitter at twitter.com/nicholebernier.

My nightstand pile is a towering and precarious place, and if it falls it will harm my children and pets. It includes both the can't-waits and really-should-reads (though I won't admit which are which). The nightstand is the place where I protect my very best intentions so they don't get lost in the weigh station that is my stack against the bedroom wall, or God forbid, the bookshelves downstairs.

These days (eyeing the stack like a dangerous animal) the bedside represents a mix of research, pleasure, and sanity:

Geraldine Brooks, *People of the Book* — I've been a fan since I first read *A Year of Wonders*, and learned that she's a graduate of the same journalism school I attended, had worked for the AP in the Mideast and then turned to fiction. She now writes from Martha's Vineyard, where she lives with her family, and her work has the mark of a journalist's intense research, whether her subject matter is the plague in 1600s England, or in this case, the history of a 1400s Haggadah, and its travels through the centuries to be found in wartime Sarajevo. I learn from her constantly.

Wallace Stegner, *Crossing to Safety* — I've read this three times before—in my 20s, 30s, and early 40s—and am brushing up on it to lead a book club discussion at my local bookstore. It's the story of two couples, their lifelong marriages and friendship, and takes a clear-eyed look at how our strengths and foibles become more forgiving and more brittle over the decades. It is one of my all-time favorite novels, and in part inspired my novel about the faces of ourselves we show and the facades we keep, even with those closest to us. Stegner won the Pulitzer for *Angle of Repose*, but this is the one that's dear to me.

Chris Bohjalian, *The Sandcastle Girls* — I love books that take me to another time, place, culture or strife; I love books that make me learn and think while being entertained, so much so that I can picture the place in my mind (as I've envisioned it) for a long time afterward. This book is doing that for me with 1915 Turkey and Syria, and the Armenian genocide. I have the opportunity to meet Chris next month, and wanted to read this first.

David Plante, *The Age of Terror* — Published in 1999, this novel about the Russian sex-slave trade came highly recommended as part of my research for my second novel. I'm a bit obsessed with the precarious world of the USSR on the verge of its disintegration, and Americans who trip into it and get stuck. I've bought **le Carré's** *The Russia House* for the same reason, but it's still in the weigh station.

Chad Harbach, *The Art of Fielding* — Three of my five children play baseball, and the sole reason the other two don't is that they are barely old enough to carry the bat. Baseball is my husband's family's game, and is as certain in my world as death and taxes. And though I'm fine with it—I'm not terribly sporty, but I like the ambience and history—I need to find literary ways to bring it closer to my heart. Even non-fans have told me this is a must-read.

Jack Kornfield, *After the Ecstasy, the Laundry* — When my heart rate gets too spiky over the to-do list—never mind the things I've forgotten to put there—this is the book that calls me in off the ledge. It's part of my marching orders to myself to take whatever happiness and wisdom is gleaned from the calm moments, and apply them to the chaos and the tedium. In the same vein, **Dalai Lama's** *The Art of Happiness*, in the weigh station.

Posted September 14, 2012.

Miranda Beverly-Whittemore

Miranda Beverly-Whittemore is the author of three novels: *New York Times* bestseller *Bittersweet* (2014), *The Effects of Light* (2005) and *Set Me Free* (2007), which won the Janet Heidinger Kafka Prize for the best book of fiction by an American woman published in 2007. A recipient of the *Crazyhorse* Fiction Prize, she lives and writes in Brooklyn and Vermont.

Visit her website, mirandabw.com/, or her Bittersweet Booklaunch Blog, wegrowmedia.com/bittersweet.

I'm in an odd space with reading at the moment. I'm just starting to write a new book, which means I have to be careful about the language and ideas coming in, because I'm easily swayable (it can throw me off course to digest something at the wrong moment of book gestation). Also, I have *Bittersweet* coming out very soon, which makes for a chicken-with-its-head-cut-off uneasiness that makes sinking into someone else's novel challenging. I guess that it's because I'm stuck in the middle of two big writing moments that I'm reading more than one book (which is unusual for me). Here's what's on my nightstand at the moment:

P.D. James, *A Taste For Death* — My mother reads everything. She got that from my grandmother, who read up until her dying day at 103 (and was hesitant to start a new book that last week of her life because she was afraid she would die before she found out the ending). I consider it to be my great fortune that my mother reads a book a day, which means she's always got a recommendation. When I was visiting my parents on a recent weekend and in need of a good, gentle read, she handed me this thick P.D. James, which used to be my aforementioned grandmother's, and said, "This is slow but it'll suck you in." I've been enjoying a chapter or two before bed, appreciating its rhythm and attention to detail. Also, the language is just fantastic in that British style and tradition.

A.S. Byatt, *Possession* — This is the third time I've read *Possession*; this time I'm reading it to help me think about the book I'm writing, which also goes back and forth in time, uncovering secrets in the present day, that are, in turn, teased out in the past. Byatt's book is such a fabulous achievement—I am always blown away by her ability to pull off the poetry! Not only is it historically *on pointe*, it has all these secrets hidden inside it, which in turn inform the story. Such an accomplishment.

Nicole C. Kear, *Now I See You* — Full disclosure: Nicole is a friend of mine. But even if I didn't know her, I would admire this new memoir tremendously for its ability to turn something seemingly tragic (her diagnosis, as a college student, with a degenerative eye disease that would render her blind) into an hysterical romp that makes you laugh until you cry. More than once I've found myself gasping for air as she describes being in labor at her Italian family's Thanksgiving, or wearing a disguise to the Gowanus Canal so she can practice using her cane incognito. I admire writers for whom humor is effortless —it's just not in my wheelhouse, but it's something I'm working on (although I find humor ends up being very shy if you try to force it).

Virginia Woolf, *To The Lighthouse* — I was having an angsty moment the other day and pulled this down from my shelf (I've read it at least a dozen times, and every time I find something new in it). Word to the wise: don't read Woolf when you're feeling blue about the state of the world! She's just so brilliant, but her darkness finds every open wound on you. Still, I haven't been able to reshelve it; it's kind of sitting there staring at me. Woolf by osmosis.

Ian McEwan, *Atonement* — Also not a great choice for a

blue day. But I thought a lot about this novel when I was writing *Bittersweet* — the idea of an Edenic place ruined by a single act — and wanted to dip back into it. I suppose this is a real indication of how I read; wanting to be back in the mood of something and then borrowing it for a short time, but not necessarily reading the whole thing from cover to cover. McEwan is currently holding hands with Woolf on my nightstand.

Posted May 9, 2014.

Doug Borsom

Doug Borsom grew up in Hinsdale, Illinois. He studied physics at Case Western Reserve University in Cleveland, but transferred to Knox College in Galesburg, Illinois to study literature, and discovered creative writing classes. He had started writing at age 12 because he thought books were powerful, so writing conferred power. He completed his MFA in fiction from the University of Iowa Writers' Workshop in 1975. "I don't think of myself as a writer," he says. "It's just something I do." After Iowa, he taught creative writing for three years at Southwest Missouri State before returning to school to study mathematics at the University of Wisconsin. For 20 years, his day job was in the computer industry. Doug lives in Pasadena and is writing a novel.

What's by my bed now:

George Orwell and more Orwell: *Down and Out in Paris and London*, *Burmese Days*, and essays — Ever since I read "How the Poor Die" some years back, I've been meaning to return to Orwell. Now I am.

Mark Twain, *Life on the Mississippi* — Another gaping hole I'm finally going to fill. And there's a tie-in with Orwell. According to Christopher Hitchens, Orwell was fascinated by Twain's depiction of the Mississippi and hoped someday to raft down it. Unfortunately, Hitchens rafted a different river first, and missed his chance.

George Bernard Shaw, *Back to Methuselah* — A socialist, hung out with Hollywood celebs, co-founded the London School of Economics, wrote a load of plays. *Back to Methuselah* is five, count 'em, five plays that cover something like 30,000 years. Shaw's plays read well, and I'm looking forward to this.

Jennie Fields, *The Age of Desire* — So many good things have been said and written about the book. And it's by Jennie Fields, a friend and admired classmate at Iowa. And it's about Edith Wharton. Three-for-three. Of course I want to read it.

Shirley Jackson, *Shirley Jackson: Novels and Stories*, edited by Joyce Carol Oates — Like all of us, I've read "The Lottery" and heard about Jackson's reputation as a master of the unsettling. In addition to publishing a new book every 17 days, Joyce Carol Oates was destined to edit this collection.

Edward Teller and **Judith Shoolery**, *Memoirs: A Twentieth-Century Journey in Science and Politics* — Teller, a brilliant Hungarian refugee (brilliance was common among them), was known as "the father of the hydrogen bomb." He relished the title and doted on his offspring. His other child was the strategic defense initiative, nicknamed the star wars space defense. What a family.

A couple recent *New Yorkers.*

Posted September 23, 2012.

David Corbett

David Corbett is the *New York Times* Notable Author of five novels, dozens of stories, numerous scripts, and too many poems. Recovering Catholic, ex-PI, one-time bar-band gypsy, his book on the craft of characterization, *The Art of Character*—"[A] writer's bible that will lead to your character's soul," Elizabeth Brundage—was published by Penguin in 2013. His latest novel, *Save By An Evil Chance*, will appear in April 2015.

Visit his website at davidcorbett.com.

A.M. Homes, *May We Be Forgiven* — As deft a balancing act between heartbreaking realism and wicked black humor as I've read outside the works of Pete Dexter (see below). An opening scene with a gutted Thanksgiving turkey, fingers dripping with meat juices, lips coated in same, and then an illicit kiss between the protagonist and his brother's wife—and it just takes off from there. Uncanny pacing for a so-called literary novel—violent and smart, and did I mention funny?

Duane Swierczynski, *The Blonde* — The reading equivalent of listening to Eddy Angel channel Link Wray. Gutsy and quick on its feet, with so many deft strokes and oddball observations and switchback plot turns, not to mention (lest we forget) the eponymous blonde who, of course, is not who she seems—a patch of red in a private spot gives her away. More to the point, she'll die if someone isn't within ten feet of her. Literally. Beat that, Salman Rushdie!

Jean de La Bruyère, *Characters* — A gift from my agent, in celebration of the publication of my book, *The Art of Character*. This is the kind of item only the French write, reminiscent of Stendhal's *De l'amour* and Flaubert's *Dictionary of Accepted Ideas*, except not as narrowly focused as the former nor as witty as the latter. A compendium of aphorisms on human nature, based liberally on the *Moral Characters of Theophrastus*.

Connie Zweig and **Jeremiah Abrams**, editors, *Meeting the Shadow: The Hidden Power of the Dark Side of Human Nature* — Jungian in bent, a much more interesting exploration of our propensity for damage than the **Mark Larrimore** volume, *The Problem of Evil*, and far less judgmental than *The Criminal Mind* by **Katherine Ramsland**, or *The Psychopathic Mind* by **Reid J. Meloy**, or as self-help sappy as *The Sociopath Next Door* by **Martha Stout**.

Don Carpenter, *Hard Rain Falling* — They just don't write books like this anymore, except maybe the work of Bonnie Jo Campbell and Donald Ray Pollock—tough and clear-eyed and human. Young men adrift and careening toward trouble in the Pacific Northwest of the late 1950s. *On the Road* meets *Fight Club* without the precious need to be important. If you're paying attention, there's no need to be transgressive. Reality will answer that call any day of the week.

Nick Reding *Methland* — A haunting look at a small Midwestern town's devastation at the hands of an insidious drug, but with an eye to the larger picture—the migratory patterns gutting rural America, the tectonic economic shifts marooning America's young, the aimless hum of hopelessness in the land.

Pete Dexter, *Spooner* — My hero. I read and weep. A male Martha Gelhorn (no, Hemingway doesn't get that nod). Sentences as clear as glass and twice as dangerous. The human condition reported with humor and heart but utterly stripped of sentiment. The driest of martinis, with a beer back. Can't get enough of this guy. Truly, deeply, I hate him.

Posted February 15, 2013.

Christi Craig

Christi Craig lives and writes in Wisconsin, working by day as a sign language interpreter and moonlighting as a writer. She is an Assistant Editor for the online journal, *Compose*, Associate Editor at *Noble/Gas Qtrly*, and leads workshops and critique groups at Red Oak Writing in Milwaukee. Her stories have appeared online and in print, and she was a finalist in *Glimmer Train*'s Family Matters Competition.

Visit her website at christicraig.com, or follow her on Twitter at twitter.com/Christi_Craig.

This is hard to admit, but I haven't always been an avid reader. There was a time when my nightstand was void of books. It was the early '80s, and I was 12 and on a mission to record the whole of Kim Carnes' "Bette Davis Eyes," index finger suspended over the pause button of my portable radio cassette player, ears locked on the DJ's voice in anticipation. I had little time to read, so focused on catching the first notes of the song that led into her raspy voice. Books were the least of my passions.

Nowadays, I listen to music on Pandora, sans DJ. I record story ideas on my iPhone rather than songs. Our house is brimming with books: by my bed, on my desk, crowding the stairs, and stacked on the dining room table.

Last summer, I fell in love with **Robert Goolrick**'s *A Reliable Wife*, a *New York Times* bestseller that opens with a great line: "It was bitter cold, the air electric with all that had not happened yet."

Electric. Then, in beautiful and concise prose, Goolrick's novel unfolds through well-chosen details, revealing a woman and a man and the wreckage of their past, the unexpected attachments they form with each other. And redemption.

I have two copies of **Patricia Ann McNair**'s book of short stories, *The Temple of Air*, and another collection of short fiction by **Erika Dreifus**, *Quiet Americans*. McNair's stories are rich in character and place, and several, like "Deer Story," left me breathless. *Quiet Americans* is much the same, full of tales about men and women searching to unravel and reconcile the complexities of their past, which for them is bound to the Holocaust.

I recently finished two books by Native American authors, *Bloodlines: Odyssey of a Native Daughter* by **Janet Campbell Hale** and *Ceremony* by **Leslie Marmon Silko**. They were on loan from the library. I picked them up in the name of research, but I was tempted to keep them for longer than allowed. I am notorious for paying fines, and I hate letting go of a good book. Hale's book is a memoir and Silko's a novel, and both speak of ties to home and family, of the urge to leave and the unrelenting drive to return if only to uncover the mystery of self.

With two young kids at home, I watch for good middle grade books and young adult novels, too, especially for my son. He just turned 12, and he's as hard a reader to please as I always was. But, he's also at a ripe age for book learning. When we find a story that piques his interest, I jump at it. Often, he lets me read it to him. Those are the books I love best, the ones he shares with me.

We laughed through **W.H. Beck**'s *Malcolm at Midnight*, which tells of a rat who pretends to be a mouse so he can live the high life of a fifth-grade class pet. The story takes off when a favorite iguana goes missing, and Malcolm becomes the prime suspect. As he sets out to clear his good name, he uncovers his true purpose in life…or his rathood. I thought fifth grade was hard; I never knew all the goings-on with class pets.

We read through all four of **Lois Lowry**'s coming-of-age stories. Sitting down with *Son*, the story of Claire, a young girl assigned to the job of birthmother, we came upon the word "insemination" within the first five minutes, and I found myself fumbling through a conversation about the birds and the bees. Lucky for me, the world Lowry creates is far more exciting than any explanation I could offer on the science of babies.

And, we survived more than 2,500 pages of **Christopher Paolini**'s *Inheritance Cycle* series about dragons and kindred spirits. When I say "we," I mean my son survived, because for the last page and a half of *Inheritance* that I read out loud, I sobbed. Paolini weaves an amazing story of relationships, especially the one between Eragon and Arya, human and elf, and I knew what was coming. I warned my son as we approached the end that I might "tear up" a bit. Then, a few lines later I had to excuse myself so I could fall apart in the bathroom. He sat shocked, jaw open, asking me if I was laughing or crying. I said, both, because technically I was in hysterics in between sobs, thinking how ridiculous that I should cry so hard over a kids' book when I knew how things would unfold but—my word—isn't that how books work? You never know when a story will grab you so hard. Once you're in, you're in, and there's no letting go, even after you've closed the cover.

A story is a story is a story. I say that in a good way. Memoir or fiction, short or long. We are bred for stories; we read them, we write them, we share them over coffee or at bedtime. Stories about place and family, redemption and love. They keep us in conversation and guide us through some new understanding of the world, even if that understanding is the fact that your mother is human and cries like a baby over the fate of a young Dragon Rider.

Talk about passionate. Who needs Kim Carnes when you have a whole world of books?

Posted February 2, 2014.

Matt Debenham

Matt Debenham is the author of *The Book of Right and Wrong*, winner of the 2009 Ohio State University Press Prize for Fiction. He is also author of two independent stories, "The Advocate" and "Challenger," both available on Amazon or on his website. His fiction has appeared in *The Pinch*, *Roanoke Review*, *Battered Suitcase*, *Painted Bride Quarterly*, and other publications. He was Peter Taylor Scholar at the Sewanee Writers' Conference, and the recipient of a Fiction Fellowship from the state of Connecticut. He blogs about writing, and has a weekly books-discussion podcast. He is available for parties.

Visit his blog at mattdebenham.com, or his podcast at whatareyoureading.libsyn.com.

My book situation is a mess, but only because my bedside situation isn't. My wife and I lack a certain amount of discipline, and compensate by doing the minimum: We take our vitamins daily, and we keep our bedside tables relatively free of clutter. So what would be stacked by my bedside is on shelves elsewhere throughout the house, from our office to the living room to the basement. (Which is where the bulk of our book collection lives. As a monster should.) And then there's what's piled up quietly in my iPad. Pulling from these various locations, here's what I've read most recently, and what's on the docket.

Deborah Levy, *Swimming Home* (iPad) — A short, dreamlike novel about a London poet and womanizer who, as a child, was a Jewish refugee during World War II. On holiday in France with his family, he's visited by a woman who claims to be his greatest fan, yet who may actually be an angel of mercy. I've developed a theory that some of the shortest, sharpest novels are written by people who didn't start out as novelists—Levy is a celebrated playwright; *Away's* **Amy Bloom** is primarily a short story writer; *City of Thieves* is by **David Benioff**, who also writes for movies and television—and I think it's because these other types of fiction writing demand compression, by definition. At any rate, Levy telegraphs the hell out of her ending, but the book is so tight and interesting and so full of narrative authority that her Chekhov's Swimming Pool is hardly a negative (someone shoots a swimming pool, is what I'm saying).

Ed Brubaker and **Sean Phillips**, *Fatale, Book 1* (office) — Something I've grown into quite a bit over the last ten years is comics. Aside from Ed Brubaker's Captain America run, I'm not much of a superhero guy, but there's an amazing amount of great non-superhero stuff out there. Some favorites: *Y: The Last Man* (**Brian K. Vaughan** and **Pia Guerra**), about an epidemic that wipes out every male on Earth—except one; *Scalped* (**Jason Aaron** and **R.M. Guéra**), which is kind of like *The Departed* on a Native American reservation; *Wasteland* (**Antony Johnston**), an incredibly well-realized post-apocalyptic epic; and anything else by the writer-artist team of **Ed Brubaker** and **Sean Phillips**. They've investigated every nook of the pulp genre, from straight hardboiled fiction (the *Criminal* series) to secret agents (*Sleeper*) to superheroes & supervillains (*Incognito*)—always with surprising plotting, sharp dialogue, and a great sense of character. (And Phillips' art feels midcentury, no matter what the setting, yet never feels static.) *Fatale*, their newest venture, is a supernatural pulp story that also has hints of being a Big Story, in terms of sweep and subject matter. Book 1 is clearly just the tip of things here, and I can imagine this story widening and deepening in the way of **Alan Moore's** *From Hell*, or **Grant Morrison's** *The Invisibles*.

Christopher Vogler, *The Writer's Journey, 3rd Edition* (office) — I teach writing in a few different settings, and I usually end up explaining concepts or ideas the way I need to understand them. *The Writer's Journey* sounds like one of those books about the importance of, I don't know, leaving your family and writing thrice daily with a purple pen, but it's subtitled *Mythic Structure for Writers*. In a nutshell? It's **Robert McKee's** *Story* without the grandiosity, plus **Joseph Campbell's** *Hero With a Thousand Faces* with lots of modern examples. It's a screenwriter's book, but I recommend a lot of those to prose writers. I've read a lot of craft books by fiction writers, and most of them are either too prescriptive or weirdly vague. (I love the novelist who says, "I don't think about plot." Very insightful!) What screen- and television writers get and express so well is that plot and character are intertwined. Vogler's book breaks this down beautifully, and if you have a hard time with plot, you may love his approach. It's a book that doesn't pretend to have invented anything new, but which frames crucial concepts in a way that's accessible and useful.

Clinton Heylin, *From the Velvets to the Voidoids: The Birth of American Punk Rock* (iPad) — As a lifelong music fan and musician, I have a weakness for rock books. They're a tough bunch: It's hard to find a great one, and even the best of them will often leave you feeling a little junk-fed, either because the stories are so gross or grim (this *is* rock & roll) or because the personalities are so, by necessity, grandiose. But I always have a rock book going, as a respite from my own work, from books I'm reading for pleasure/edification, or from books I'm reading for teaching. *From the Velvets to the Voidoids* manages the neat trick of almost never overstating its case. The number-one problem with a lot of rock books is that they feel like they're constantly justifying their own existence, as though the author has to constantly remind you why Led Zeppelin or Elvis Costello was *the* most important act of all time. Heylin sidesteps this because he knows he can: Punk's impact is kind of unquestionable. Instead, Heylin uses a combination of journalistic prose and first-person accounts to just tell what happened, between New York, Cleveland, Detroit, and Los

Angeles. The scope keeps it interesting and nicely democratic. The birth of punk in the U.S. is a great story, and Heylin has given it the most comprehensive telling to date.

Salman Rushdie, *Midnight's Children* (living room) — A friend and co-worker gave this to me years ago. Like 17 years ago. He'd just read it and thought I'd love it. He gave it specifically to me, and I did not read it. There it sits on my living room shelves, not mocking me, but judging me. Shaming me. This year's gonna be the year. (Note: it wasn't! *Midnight's Children* still sits there in quiet judgment.)

Shalom Auslander, *Hope: A Tragedy* (iPad) — Here's what I'm reading next: A novel about a troubled, unmoored Jewish man who finds an old woman claiming to be Anne Frank living in his attic. In modern-day upstate New York. Come on, who could resist this premise?

Herman Melville, *Moby-Dick* (basement; iPad) — If you listen to my books-discussion podcast, WHAT ARE YOU READING?, you will know that I have recently begun reading this book, having avoided it all my life, and yet I am still barely churning through it. I love it every time I pick it up, and yet the act of picking it up always feels like I'm returning to the piano I know I was supposed to have been practicing for the day's lesson. (Which reminds me: I forgot to start taking piano lessons 30 years ago.) The copy I read now is on my iPad, but I started on a physical copy borrowed from my parents' house. That one is a hardback from the 1940s, and I stopped reading it because I didn't want to damage it. OR SO I WILL KEEP TELLING MYSELF.

Posted May 24, 2013.

Julia Fierro

Julia Fierro's debut novel, *Cutting Teeth*, was recently included in *Library Journal's* "Spring Best Debuts" and on "Most Anticipated Books of 2014 lists by *HuffPost Books*, *The Millions*, *Flavorwire*, *Brooklyn Magazine*, and *Marie Claire*. Julia's work has been published, or is forthcoming, in *Poets & Writers*, *Glamour*, and other publications, and she has been profiled in *L Magazine*, *The Observer* and *The Economist*.

In 2002, she founded The Sackett Street Writers' Workshop, and what started as eight writers meeting in her Brooklyn kitchen has grown into a creative home for over 2000 writers. A graduate of The Iowa Writers' Workshop, where she was a Teaching-Writing Fellow, Julia currently teaches the Post-MFA workshops at Sackett Street.

She can be found on her website at juliafierro.com/author, on Twitter at twitter.com/JuliaFierro, or on Facebook at facebook.com/juliafierroauthor.

My bedside table is an embarrassment of riches when it comes to books this spring, particularly advance copies of forthcoming novels and story collections, most by writers who, like me, have books being released this season. We swap books, which makes it extra fun to cheer each author on as he or she nears their book's publication date. Needless to say, I am reading as fast as I can to keep up with all the amazing books showing up at my doorstep. Here are just a few stacked on my night table.

Robin Black, *Life Drawing* — Robin Black's hotly anticipated debut has the gorgeous prose of a literary novel and the momentum of a thriller. The tension Black creates between the novel's four main characters sizzles just under the surface of the book's quiet, and often mesmerizing, tone. I was up late several nights in a row turning pages, nervous and excited to see just what would happen, but wanting to slow down to enjoy the many snippets of emotionally intelligent wisdom Black filters through the characters' perspectives. I dog-eared practically every other page so I could share a line here or there with my husband. *Life Drawing* is a bravely honest depiction of the complexities of marriage—the need, the betrayal, the love and heartbreak. It is definitely a book I will read again, and I'm confident I'll find new treasures.

Mira Jacob, *The Sleepwalker's Guide to Dancing* — I'm halfway through Mira Jacob's debut novel and am already certain it is going to be loved by many readers this summer. Funny, clever, smartly told, entertaining, beautifully written, and with a cast of characters that reminds you why the experience of humanity is both hilarious and heartbreaking, *The Sleepwalker's Guide to Dancing* is a must read. The novel's story jumps seamlessly from India to America as one family's fascinating story is revealed. I love a fast-paced read that is filled with fun characters. Mira's debut is a perfect pick for a fun and thought-provoking book-club discussion.

Miranda Beverly-Whittemore, *Bittersweet* — I just saw that Miranda was the last author to post a "Books By The Bed" list and I am lucky to call her a friend—plus our novels launched on the same day, so we are "book birthday twins." *Bittersweet* is going to be one of the biggest books of the summer. It is a true page-turner. I was up late-late-night three nights in a row reading it. And my pulse was definitely racing! A contemporary coming-of-age story with a suspenseful gothic-flavored twist, *Bittersweet* follows a young woman, Mabel Dagmar, over a summer spent at a sprawling Vermont estate. As Mabel falls in and out of love with the mysterious blue-blooded Winslow clan, so does the reader.

Jeff Vandermeer, *Annihilation (Southern Reach Trilogy)* — I picked up a copy of the first book in Vandermeer's trilogy while at Word Brooklyn bookstore (where I was signing copies of *Cutting Teeth*, exciting!). I love a great genre-bender, and although I'm only 50 pages into the novel, I know *Annihilation*, and the rest of the trilogy are going to hook me. Part sci-fi, part psychological thriller and part literary, the novel is set in a mysterious region known as Area X and follows a team of researchers on an expedition into the forbidden zone. I wish I had it with me *right now* (its on my bedside table, of course) so I could keep reading.

Mary Pope Osborne, *The Magic Treehouse Series* — My six-year-old son loves this series and it is a perfect blend of fantasy, adventure, and history that keeps both him and his four-year-old sister entertained. I often have the latest book in the series on my bedside table. Right now, we are reading book #19, *Tigers at Twilight*. The storyline of the series follows a brother and sister who are, luckily, the same ages as my son and daughter. They discover a magical treehouse in the woods filled with books. On each visit to the treehouse they choose a different book that transports them to a magical land, often one associated with a historical period. We've watched Jack and Annie travel to Camelot, to an ancient Roman chariot race, and to Pompeii. They also visit faraway lands—the Arctic, the forests of India, and Australia. It is a fascinating chapter-book series perfect for young readers, and for parents to read to children preschool age and up.

Rick Atkinson, *The Day of Battle: The War In Sicily and Italy, 1943-44* — Finally, I'm always listening to an audiobook, whether on my walk to the Writer's Space to work, as I'm knitting, or as I'm lying in bed waiting to fall asleep. Like many avid readers, I've always been a bit of an insomniac, even as a child hiding with a flashlight and a book under my bedcovers after lights out. My current audiobook is the second book in Rick Atkinson's incredible nonfiction WWII *The Liberation Trilogy, The Day of Battle: The War in Sicily* *and Italy, 1943-44*. My father was 8 years old and living with his family on the rocky hills of the Amalfi Coast when the Allies liberated Southern Italy. His stories about how his entire village hid in the caves for three weeks as Allied bombs, launched from the sea, rained down on them day after day, are incredible. I'm reading Rick Atkinson's meticulously researched and compassionately told book to fill in many of the gaps in my father's story, so that I can, someday, write about that devastating scene myself. The description of the countless Allied lives lost due to mismanagement and rashness, mostly as a result of the competition between the American and British generals, is mind-boggling. Now, I truly understand how the follies of war can destroy humanity in such massive numbers. This trilogy is a must for all readers, and the narrator on the audio version does a fantastic job.

Posted May 16, 2014.

Kathie Giorgio

Kathie Giorgio's fourth book, a novel titled *Rise From The River*, will be released in 2015. Two novels, *The Home For Wayward Clocks* and *Learning To Tell (A Life)Time*, and a short story collection, *Enlarged Hearts*, have all been released by Main Street Rag. Kathie's short stories and poems have appeared in more than 100 literary magazines and in many anthologies.

Kathie lives in Waukesha, Wisconsin, with her husband, mystery writer Michael Giorgio, their daughter, Olivia, and an even number of beagles and cats.

She is founder and director of AllWriters' Workplace & Workshop, an international studio offering online and on-site classes in all genres and abilities of creative writing. Check it out at allwritersworkshop.com.

Follow her on Facebook at: facebook.com/pages/Author-Kathie-Giorgio/111089342285878, and Twitter at twitter.com/KathieGiorgio.

It's been a horrible winter in Wisconsin. Subzero temps, snow amounts more than 20 inches beyond average. As a result, my bedside table, which normally supports a lot of books, currently sports a bright red humidifier. It's pretty, it tries to throw summer moisture into the air, and I glare at it every night, because I can't haul it into bed with me, open it, and give myself a few words before sleep.

However, rescue is on the way! I leave soon to be a featured reader and to teach a class in North Carolina, and then I'm scooting over to Myrtle Beach in South Carolina for a week of rest and writing. I don't have clothes amassed yet to pack, but I do have a stack of books that will grace my hotel bedside table. And the sand on the beach. And the white plastic tables poolside. And the restaurant table as I head out to eat. Oh, paradise!

What am I bringing with me?

Kelly Cherry, *A Kind of Dream: Stories* — A newly released book of short stories. When I left for college, I first studied at the knee of Kelly Cherry. Her work has always been full of impact and sharp loveliness. One of the things I love the most about Cherry's work is the combination of ambition with the ability to reach every reader. Cherry's fiction is intelligent and deep-digging, yet it doesn't carry with it any arrogance. Because this is a collection of short stories, I expect to read a story, then dip in the ocean, read another, then dip in the pool. It's a multi-purpose carry-with-me-everywhere kind of book.

Lorrie Moore, *Bark: Stories* — A newly released book of short stories. I've read Lorrie Moore for years, and her stories, in particular, are often the type that make me fold the book to my chest and stare reverently at the ceiling for a few minutes before I continue to the next page. I'm not as impressed with her two novels, but her stories, like Cherry's, contain the perfect amount of bite and sigh. Dark humor that makes me laugh even as I grieve, or the exposure of a taboo topic…all can be found in Moore's work. She was first introduced to me by a writing mentor, Ellen Hunnicutt, who said, "I read her book and had to go to a reading. Lorrie Moore is beautiful as well. So she's talented, sharp, and gorgeous. Man, you just have to hate that." I've compensated for this by never looking at Moore's photos. Well, okay, I glimpse. But then I focus only on her words. Yes, Moore is beautiful. But her words are even more so.

Laura Kasischke, *Mind of Winter* — Her new novel. It comes out a scant three days before I leave. I have it preordered and I hope to heaven it gets here. Kasischke's work is dark and engrossing and she is likely what I will be reading when I have an uninterrupted chunk of time. Instead of dessert, she will be my after-dinner reward. Once you sink into Kasischke, you can't leave any time soon. She has this way of reaching out and grabbing you by the throat, pulling you into her work as a very willing prisoner. And again, it is the unexpected harmonies that move me. Her work is often described as disturbing (so is mine!), but it's so beautifully and lyrically written that each sentence requires an homage of admiration. Stringing words together is one thing; making them sing is another. Reading Laura Kascishke is like attending a perfect concert. I know I will be fully absorbed. It better get here!

I like to read poetry before I go to sleep and if it wasn't for the humidifying monster on my bed, I would likely have at least two poetry books there. Consequently, two poets are climbing into my suitcase. Poetry before bed feels right to me – it can adjust itself to my level of sleepiness. Poetry is like the reverse of a snooze alarm. I can slap a page and get just a bit more, and then roll over to go to sleep, happy, contented. When I say words put me to sleep, I mean it in the best possible way. I'm not bored; but I am lulled, soothed, amazed, and I go to sleep, hugging that which I love the most in this world. So coming with me are **Susan Elbe** and **Max Garland**.

Susan Elbe, *The Map of What Happened* — Elbe's poetry is elegant and stirring and, most important, accessible. I hate poetry that makes me feel stupid because it attempts to be lofty or otherworldly, so buried in imagery that all real meaning is gone. Elbe's poetry taps me on the shoulder and while I read of her experiences, that same poetic finger points out the map of my own memories and brings forth events long forgotten. I find myself humming while I read Elbe; she is a quilted sampler of the past and the present. I read her, I drift into me, I read her, I drift into me. I know that when I close the book and settle into the pillow, I will feel comforted and in good company.

Max Garland, *The Postal Confessions* — Max is Wisconsin's current state Poet Laureate. And he used to be a mailman. This combination just makes me laugh out loud. It's that incongruity that Max brings to his poetry. Poems about mail routes, baseball, school dances, old trucks, front porches, seagulls and dogs. Reading Max is like coming home. I plan to read his book on the last few days of my trip, and especially on that last night before re-entering the real world and my own Wisconsin. I know Max will make me homesick, making my return to this state, even if it's still cold and snowy, most welcome.

Hopefully by the time I get there, the damn humidifier can be packed away.

Posted March 28, 2014.

Erica Goss

Erica Goss is the Poet Laureate of Los Gatos, California, and the host of Word to Word, a show about poetry. She is the author of *Wild Place* (2012) and *Vibrant Words: Ideas and Inspirations for Poets* (2014). She won the 2011 Many Mountains Moving Poetry Contest and was nominated for the Pushcart Prize in 2010 and 2013. She writes *The Third Form*, a column about video poetry, for Connotation Press. Recent work appears in *Lake Effect*, *The Red Wheelbarrow*, *Passager*, *Main Street Rag*, *Pearl*, *Rattle*, *Wild Violet*, and *Comstock Review*, among others.

Visit Erica's website at: ericagoss.com.

Whenever my husband is away, I put books on his side of the bed. It makes me feel less lonely. Recently, **Margaret Atwood**'s *MaddAddam* filled that empty place next to me. This is the third in her series that started with *Oryx and Crake* and *The Year of the Flood*.

Atwood creates a world in these three books that is like ours, but tragically skewed. In the first book, the world she describes is off by a few inches; those inches become miles by the second book. The distance humanity——or what's left of humanity——travels by *MaddAddam* is full circle, back to the starting point, but with a few leftover oddities from the near past such as pigs with human brains and fluorescent butterflies. A couple of memorable quotes: "In dreams there is no irony" and "His smile had that Botox look, as if it was a product of nerve damage."

I'm a poet, and I read fiction and non-fiction when I need a break from poetry. I'm re-reading *Dakota: A Spiritual Geography* by **Kathleen Norris**. This is the second time I've re-read this book. Not many books hold up to this many re-readings, but *Dakota* is one of them. Here's a quote from the chapter titled "Cana": "Living in a town so small that, as one friend puts it, the poets and ministers have to hang out together has its advantages." And: "It's hard to talk about western Dakota without mentioning Jell-O. A salad, in local parlance, is a dish made with Jell-O." I have clear, colorful memories from childhood of picnic tables loaded with Jell-O "salads"—marshmallows, sliced fruit, and God knows what else suspended in artificially flavored gelatin. Norris makes the great empty land of South Dakota—she calls it the "outback of America"—seem as interesting and relevant as our cities. "What does status mean in a place so at odds with American society?" she asks.

I've had **Ursula Hegi**'s *Stones from the River* by my bed for months. I'm re-reading it slowly; sometimes a week goes by and I've only consumed half a chapter. When I read this book, I feel like I'm reading my history: my grandfather was born in Düsseldorf, the same town as Hegi. The river of the title is the Rhine; a few years ago I stood with my feet in the cold water of that river and thought about the suffering of the war years, which my mother and her family endured. As I stood there deep in thought, some people rushed up from the shore and told me not to get too close. "The Rhine is not safe," they said. "The water runs fast. Just last week a man drowned here." The Rhine is where Trudi, the main character, goes to be alone, to get some peace from the terrible things that happen in her village. Something terrible happens to her there too, something that has nothing to with the war, but symbolizes dominance of the strong over the weak. Trudi, a dwarf, knows that she is considered "unfit to live," "weak," and "deformed," yet she is one of the few people in her village who sees things as they really are.

The Book of Jonah by **Joshua Max Feldman** is next to my bed in the waiting-to-read category. I'm eager to dive into a book that asks the question: "How can we explain the unexplainable?" The book is a modern re-telling of the biblical story of Jonah. I enjoyed *The Red Tent* by **Anita Diamant**, a re-telling of the story of Jacob through the eyes of his daughter, Dinah, so I'm looking forward to this version of

Jonah. Bible stories, re-told and re-imagined, interest me, as do new renditions of Greek mythologies, Shakespeare's plays, Grimm's fairy tales and other classics from the past. They deserve new audiences and new interpretations.

I reach into **Adrienne Rich**'s last book, *Tonight No Poetry Will Serve*, when my brain craves the zing that only poetry delivers. I keep forgetting to re-shelve it with my other books; hence, it sits under the big, heavy novels on my nightstand, modest and slim. I love that quality about poetry books: their size belies their power. Rich's "Axel" poems mystify and intrigue: Axel Avakar is a "fictive poet, counter-muse, brother," according to the title page. I like the idea of an imaginary person to address in poetry, an alter ego perhaps, a "counter-muse" who is the opposite gender. Here is "Axel, darkly seen, in a glass house":

> And could it be I saw you
> under a roof of glass
> in trance
>
> could it be   was passing
> by and would translate
>
> too late the strained flicker
> of your pupils   your
> inert gait   the dark
>
> garb of your reflection
> in that translucent place
>
> could be I might have
> saved you   still
> could   or would   ?

Posted March 21, 2014.

Jimin Han

Jimin Han's writing can be found in a variety of places, including NPR's "Weekend America," *The Rumpus, The Good Men Project*, *KoreanAmericanStory*, *Kartika Review*, HTMLGIANT, and *The Nuyorasian Anthology*. She teaches at the Writing Institute, Sarah Lawrence College.

Follow her on Twitter at twitter.com/jiminhanwriter, or her blog at notesfromstonebarn.tumblr.com.

I love to browse in used book shops. The week I was asked to put together a list of books by my bed, I found myself in Peekskill, New York, about half an hour from where I live. It was one of those balmy summer days when I met a friend of mine, the playwright Deborah Zoe Laufer, for coffee while we waited for our children who were in one of those camp programs. We took a walk around town and happened upon two used book stores. I think the women working in one of the bookstores in particular didn't want their books sold. They were rather cranky about parting with them, and I can relate to that because you could see they loved them that much. At the same time, giving a book to a friend and receiving one in return that was read and loved has a particular spirit that I support. The only problem is I can't go back and see the parts I underlined/circled so it's a love/hate thing for me. (I'll never get over loaning **Joan Didion's** *Slouching Towards Bethlehem*—which I got signed by her by working up the nerve to approach her at a reading at Barnard—to a friend who lost it. Lesson: don't lend anything you can't afford to lose). That day's trip to Peekskill added books to the first six listed below, which were already in a pile on the floor by my bed:

Don Lee, *The Collective* — I'm a fan. Loved his previous books. Excited to see this new one just out and Kindled it immediately. Also curious because it's about a group of students, and I've written a novel about a similar time period with that age group (very different issues though).

Lidia Yuknavitch, *The Chronology of Water* — Ran into the mother of my daughter's preschool friend in Katonah who thanked me for posting a *Dear Sugar* article on Facebook because it led her to other things to read, namely this memoir by Yuknavitch. "About our bodies and ourselves. Read it and then we'll talk," she said. So I promised her I would.

Karen Russell, *Swamplandia!* — I liked the first couple of pages and had heard about it from other writers. I wanted to understand what they were talking about.

Natasha Trethewey, *Native Guard* — Because she's the Poet Laureate and I'll read poetry anytime. And because Trethewey chose a friend of mine's poetry collection for publication, one of those contests, and I'm a fan of his work.

Linda Rodriguez, *Every Last Secret* — I like what she says on Twitter. She makes insightful, cogent political comments and writes for numerous blogs, like *The Stiletto Gang*. I had the honor of meeting her at AWP in Boston and she generously pulled me into a lunch with **Joy Castro**, author of *Nearer Home*, *Hell or High Water*, and *Island of Bones*, among many others. Linda's a powerhouse, writing as much as she does and still finding time to support other writers.

Victoria M. Johnson, *The Substitute Bride* — I was captivated by the title. So many questions came to mind. What were the circumstances that would lead to a wedding like this? What's the love story behind it? I'm a sucker for a good love story. Really, any love story. Victoria is another person I met on Twitter who reached out to me and who I appreciate so much for her kindness and creative spirit.

Anne Enright, *The Gathering* — A close friend of mine

recommended it. It opens with a haunting lyrical voice that pulled me right in. The protagonist returns home after the death of her brother.

William Styron, *Darkness Visible* — I've been afraid to read a book by as powerful a writer as Styron about depression. I've had my own battles with it enough to know that I didn't need to follow in his footsteps. I was relieved to find that the clarity of his thoughts in this memoir kept the murk and threatening whirlpool of depression at bay.

A.R. Ammons, editor, *Best American Poetry 1994* — I didn't get to take a class with Archie Ammons when I was at school even though I loved his work (he was on leave at the time). And somehow I missed this *Best American* collection, and it was one of the few poetry books in that same Peekskill bookstore.

Caroline Hwang, *In Full Bloom* — I love to read books by Asian American writers, remembering a time before the Internet when I only knew of a few.

Sok-kyong Kang, **Chi-won Kim**, and **Chong-hui O**, *Words of Farewell: Stories by Korean Women Writers* — A special book that is always by my bed, a collection of Korean women writers in translation. It has my favorite short story in it, by Sok-kyong Kang, entitled "A Room in the Woods." It's a story told by a woman who has lost her sister during the pro-democracy movement in Korea. I visited Korea during that same time period and have tried to write about it numerous times. There are books that I find myself returning to time and time again and this is one of them.

Posted July 13, 2012.

Sally Koslow

Sally Koslow is the author of four novels: *The Widow Waltz*, her most recent, released in 2014; *With Friends Like These*, chosen by Target for its Emerging Writers category; *The Late, Lamented Molly Marx*, a Target Book Pick and a bestseller in German; and her debut, *Little Pink Slips*, inspired by being editor-in-chief of *McCall's Magazine*, which was taken over by a TV celebrity. Sally is also the author of a recent non-fiction book, *Slouching Toward Adulthood: How to Let Go So Your Kids Can Grow Up*, which NBC optioned for sit-com development. Her books have been published in a dozen other languages—Chinese is her favorite—and her essays appear in the anthologies *DIRT: The Quirks, Habits and Passions of Keeping House,* and *Wedding Cake for Breakfast*, as well as in magazines such as *More*, *Real Simple*, and *O*, the Oprah magazine, and on many websites.

She hopes you will visit her website at: sallykoslow.com/content/index.asp. Follow her on Twitter at twitter.com/sallykoslow, or join her Author Page on Facebook at facebook.com/SallyKoslowAuthor.

I like to write, but more than that, I like to read.

There is such a pile of books next to my bed I can barely find my glasses and Vitamin D. I constantly reshuffle my queue, depending on what needs to be finished for my book clubs—I'm in two, what's due at the library, what I can't wait to read because a friend is the author, what manuscript needs a blurb, and what jumped to the front of the line because it's shrieking "Read me first!" My favorite books are so rich in language, ideas, imagination and complex characters that they send me running to my Mac, inspired to write. A great book is a pollinating bee.

If I weren't writing this blog, I'd be finishing *The Woman Upstairs* by **Claire Messud**. This novel deserves all its praise.

Nora Eldridge, a Boston teacher, breaks your heart as she succumbs to the charms of a couple and child who irrevocably change her life over the course of one year. Nora is smart, insightful and funny, a perfect protagonist.

Messud is the wife of *New Yorker* royalty, book critic James Wood, whose essay about *The Patrick Melrose Novels* by **Edward St. Aubyn** convinced my book club to read the first of five connected novels. Once I finished *Never Mind,* I could not stop from gobbling up the next wickedly funny four. The series dissects a dysfunctional upper-class English dynasty. My favorite is about a weekend bender that Patrick, the books' anti-hero, goes on when he visits New York City for his father's funeral. "I think my mother's death is the best thing to happen to me since," Patrick eventually says, "…since my father's death."

My book club has committed to reading books that have stood the test of time. My favorites have been *Moon Tiger* by **Penelope Lively**; *The Pursuit of Love* by **Nancy Mitford**; *Lolita* by **Vladimir Nabokov**; *Portrait of a Lady* by **Henry James**; *Gilead* **by Marilynne Robinson**; *The Finkler Question* by **Howard Jacobson**; *The Girls of Slender Means* by **Muriel Spark**; and *The Sea, The Sea* by **Iris Murdoch**. I've chided our group about the fact that we read too many Brits and too many men. We'll fix that.

Frequently, I have a book on my table that relates to the Holocaust. A recent discovery was *The Life of Objects* by **Susanna Moore**, which was spare, haunting and elegant. The story is told from the viewpoint of a naïve young Irish woman who joins a household of German art collectors, ostensibly to make fine lace. Maeve Palmer is free to leave her employers as the war progresses, yet as Maeve's awareness of Nazi hypocrisy and atrocity grows, so does her loyalty to these proud yet surprisingly sympathetic aristocrats. Over the last few years I've also thoroughly enjoyed *City of Women* by **David Gillham**, *Those Who Save Us* by **Jenna Blum**, *The Zookeeper's Wife* by **Diane Ackerman**, *Every Man Dies Alone* by **Hans Fallada**, and the classic, *The Book Thief* by **Markus Zusak**.

I love a book that gives insights into another culture, especially contemporary Israel. Two of the most fascinating in the last few years have been *To the End of the Land* by **David Grossman**, about love and loyalty between a triangle of friends during the years 1967 to 2000, and *Second Person Singular* by **Sayed Kashua**, which allowed me to see the country from an Arab perspective.

In addition to writing, I teach at Sarah Lawrence College's Writing Institute and through the New York Writers Workshop. The number of would-be memoirists amazes me. I often point them to a superb memoir I enjoyed years ago—*Stuffed: Adventures of a Restaurant Family* by **Patricia Volk**. Now the author has written *Shocked: My Mother, Schiaparelli, and Me.* Its shocking pink cover is calling me.

I couldn't complete this list without mentioning *Time and Again*, **Jack Finney's** tale of magical realism, because it was published the year I moved to Manhattan, and forever changed the way I see New York City. That's what good books do, change the way you see the world.

Posted May 31, 2013.

Claire Lombardo

Claire Lombardo is a fiction writer hailing originally from Oak Park, Illinois. She has a BA in English from the University of Illinois at Chicago and she studied graduate-level social work at the University of Illinois at Urbana-Champaign. She writes short stories and is currently at work on her first novel.

To sample some of Claire's fiction and essays, visit her website at clairelombardo.com.

Save for two, all of the books currently by my bed are books I've read before. I am a re-reader. I have a rotation of several books to which I return when I'm feeling lonely or uninspired or underwhelmed or disillusioned because I know (if enough time has passed between readings) that I'm sure to be pulled headlong into a great story that reminds me of all that great literature can do for its reader. I feel about these books—there is a handful (a huge handful; the hands of Goliath)—the way I assume most people feel about old friends: they make me nostalgic; they make me emote; they make me remember earlier times in my life (usually times when I was way more embarrassing than I am now). I reread books when I'm sad, or when I'm creatively stunted, or when I'm forced on a nightly basis to read dull, atrociously-written textbooks about mental disorders and I'm feeling resentful. Now that I'm no longer studying English, I make it my mission to spend at least 30 minutes each night reading something for pleasure. So there has been a lot of rereading happening lately.

Maria Semple, *This One is Mine* — I'm obsessed. I read Semple's *Where'd You Go, Bernadette?* earlier this year, finished it in the middle of my sociology class (because stylishly-disguised Kindles are hands-down the greatest 21st-century invention for a rogue student like myself), and immediately read it again. And then I did the same with her debut novel. *This One is Mine* is delightful. Semple's characters are intricately *human* in a way that writers can't always achieve, and she has a hilarious mastery of dialogue. Her writing makes me feel like things are going to be okay in the world: probably not in an overt way, and probably not all at once, but things will be fine. We're all crazy; we're all lost; and we're all going to find our way.

Charles Baxter, *Believers* — Charles Baxter rocks my world. I'm the baby of the family, and my three older sisters (all English majors) are 8, 10, and 11 years my senior. This was primarily a blessing, especially because I was exposed to great books much earlier than I otherwise would have been. *The Feast of Love* was one of the first adult novels I ever read (and I use that qualifier in a purely literary sense), when I was probably 15, and Baxter has remained since then one of my very favorite writers. I'm rereading *Believers* both to help me hone my own craft of short-story writing and because *duh*. Baxter has a great gift for making the Midwest seem interesting. *Or*, in absentia, making it seem okay that the Midwest is inherently *not* interesting.

Adam Langer, *Crossing California* — Unless you have lived in Chicago, worked in Chicago, or read *Crossing California*, you cannot begin to understand how strange a city Chicago really is. I last read this magnificent homage to my hometown when I was in high school, so I'm very excited to be starting it again. Langer is absolutely spot-on with his depictions of middle-income class warfare, the constantly torturous lives of high schoolers, and the (tragically) hilarious politics of Chicago. He has a head-spinning, meticulous attention to detail and an acute, highly amusing cultural radar. This is a dense book, not very dialogue-heavy, and you don't want to miss a single word because Adam Langer is so, so smart. Lest you were ever curious what it was like to grow up in West Rogers Park in the late '70s, this book will answer all questions.

Ayelet Waldman, *Love and Other Impossible Pursuits* — I've got a serious thing for stories of quiet desperation, especially as they pertain to families and motherhood. I'm not completely sure where this comes from, as I'm not a mother myself, but it's a topic I find myself exploring in my own writing as well. Waldman is a master, one of my very, very favorite contemporary writers. I'm rereading this book, too, and it's just the absolute worst because whenever anyone asks what I'm reading and what it's about I go completely blank. In this case, I usually end up saying something like, "Well, it's kind of about SIDS, I guess. But only a little." And this doesn't even begin to do it justice; what I really should say is "It's about love and fate and legacy and family and the way all of those things clash and overlap and let us down and reinforce our faith in humanity and *it's so good*, trust me." I'll try to remember that for the next time someone asks.

Doris Lessing, *The Fifth Child* — I am the fifth child. This terrifying book is more or less the story of my life. This has been beside me for a few months, because I had to stop reading out of fear. It's essentially the story of a young couple that falls in love and moves into a giant house with the shared dream of having a bunch of kids—*which is essentially my origin story.* I won't spoil the ending for you, because I can't, because I had to put this down immediately after *the fifth child* was born (appropriating, as an infant, such troubling adjectives as "muscular" and "yellow") and have been too afraid to pick it up since.

D.T. Max, *Every Love Story is a Ghost Story: A Life of David Foster Wallace* — Most biographies are anathema to the very core of my spirit, but this one reads almost like a novel. Oh boy, do I wish that David Foster Wallace were still with us. I wish, additionally, that he still lived in Urbana, because I think this place really benefited from his presence.

Mark Salzman, *True Notebooks: A Writer's Year at Juvenile Hall* — This is a book that—gasp!—actually bridges the gap between what I love and what I'm studying. I whine a lot about my halcyon days as an English major (it must get pretty annoying), and a friend from my program presented me with this book after I decided to do some research on creative writing therapy. I pretty much had to check my writerly hat at the door when I entered social work school, but this story—of Salzman's experience teaching a writing workshop in a high-risk juvenile detention facility in LA—highlights the value of art and creativity in the therapeutic process. It's heartbreaking and delightful and particularly inspiring for my woeful, meandering twentysomething self as I try to figure out what it is I want to do with my life.

Posted October 11, 2013.

Tom Molanphy

Tom Molanphy earned his MFA in Creative Writing from the University of Montana. His most recent book, *Loud Memories Of A Quiet Life*, was published by OutPost19. He freelances for 10Best/Travel Media Group at *USA Today*. His short story "Of Subareas and Public Bathrooms" was included in the California Prose Directory, 2013. Tom teaches creative writing, composition, and journalism at the Academy of Art University. He also taught composition at the University of San Francisco, and he occasionally tutors at 826 Valencia in San Francisco, helping young people with their reading and writing.

Read an excerpt from his latest at outpost19.com/LoudMemories.

I have a flashlight, a copper pipe and a pair of wax earplugs near my bed for blackouts, security and unwanted noise. I keep **Flannery O'Connor**, **John McPhee** and **Gretel Ehrlich** within reach for the same reasons.

For blackouts:

Flannery O'Connor, *A Good Man Is Hard To Find* —

> "I call myself The Misfit," he said, "because I can't make what all I done wrong fit what all I gone through in punishment."

I heard the Cistercian monk Brother Robert read "A Good Man Is Hard To Find" in 1989. I was one of fourteen high school seniors at Cistercian Prep in Irving, Texas. Most of us had spent eight years at the all-boys Catholic high school. All of us were one month from liberation, one month until years of uniforms, standing at attention, and rigid Hungarian-monk-Middle-Ages-discipline would be replaced by college freedoms. We were starving for new experiences and certain the small school in the middle of Texas had nothing left to offer.

Brother Robert knew this. But even his sharp sarcasm and caustic threats couldn't revive any desire to learn in us. Overweight and sweating underneath his thick monk's robes, Brother Robert flipped open O'Connor's paperbacked and peacocked short story collection.

"Today I'll read 'A Good Man Is Hard To Find' by Flannery O'Connor."

I pillowed my forearms on my desk and snuggled in. When Brother Robert read in class, I sensed it was more for him than for us. He appreciated the sound and fury of language in a way that he couldn't explain but was compelled to share. My mind wandered outside onto the burnt lawn and bright sunshine and dusty scrub oaks.

The idea of a grandmother on a road trip with her family did not grip me. I tried to shake loose completely, but something about her foolhardy certainty kept reining me in. What nabbed my interest was the voice. These were the Dallas housewives I had heard prattling on in the aisles of Safeway. They were coming off a page and through the mouth of a fat monk.

How did O'Connor do this? By the time the Misfit showed up, my reality had been replaced by O'Connor's fiction. I do my best to never let that moment get blacked out.

For security:

John McPhee, *Assembling California* —

> In San Francisco (in 1989), the tremors will last fifteen seconds. As the ground violently shakes and the sand boils of the Marina discharge material from the liquefying depths, the things they spit up include tarpaper and bits of redwood—the charred remains of houses from the

earthquake of 1906.

I moved to San Francisco in 2000 and into a Victorian four blocks up from Haight-Ashbury. The #33 MUNI rumbled past my bedroom each night, close enough to shake my bed. After four months of these tremors, I thought I had adjusted to the buses rumbling by.

One night I woke up to a terrific shaking. I was groggy and believed it was two buses, one after another. I clutched my comforter for stability. At morning coffee, my roommates informed me I had half-experienced my first San Francisco earthquake.

McPhee keeps me connected to the faults I still sleep on. I read McPhee's dense texts slowly, sometimes falling asleep, but always with a smile. My glacial reading pace leaves its mark. His grip on the California terrain is as smooth and certain as a copper pipe. When my bed shakes, now I know why.

For unwanted noise:

Gretel Ehrlich, *The Solace of Open Spaces* —

> We Americans are great on fillers, as if what we have, what we are, is not enough. We have a cultural tendency towards denial, but, being affluent, we strangle ourselves with what we can buy. We have only to look at our houses we build to see we build against space, the way we drink against pain and loneliness. We fill up space as if it were a pie shell, with things whose opacity further obstructs our ability to see what is already there.

I live in Daly City, a suburb of San Francisco. It's as similar to San Francisco as Walker Percy's Covington was to New Orleans. Daly City is much quieter than San Francisco, but the earplugs on my night stand are necessary insurance.

Quiet has become rare and valuable. With constant chatter

all around us, Armageddon could come and go while we have our heads bowed to our Blackberries.

Ehrlich's essay reminds me to covet and hoard quiet moments. She only puts down the words that matter, respecting both the Spartan style of E. B. White ("Omit needless words") and a timeless Zen philosophy ("Only break the silence if you can improve upon it"). Her writing reminds me that only in quiet does the imagination have space to act.

Posted November 1, 2013.

Melody Murray

Melody Murray is a fiction writer and essayist. Born and raised in the DC Metropolitan area, she followed a BA in biology and English from the University of Pennsylvania by teaching science and English in the Peace Corps. After two years in southern Africa and two years back in Virginia, she is looking forward to staying put in San Diego.

There are no books by my bed. Well none of *my* books are by the bed. The three shelves above the beside sturdy wooden dresser house my boyfriend's mix of applied dynamics and engineering tomes, the works of C.S. Lewis, family photos, and handmade candles from Swaziland. When I moved to San Diego from Virginia, I agreed to bring only essentials for the next few weeks. The movers would ship everything else and store it until we found a home base for our new lives.

I limited myself to the three books closest to my bed the night before the move and they have sustained me through my uprooting. There is room on the dresser by the bed, but I keep my books closer still—under pillows, nestled in between the comforter and the duvet cover, and poking from the narrow space between the dresser and the bed.

Edward P. Jones, *All Aunt Hagar's Children* — Because his stories are home to me. He was the first author who found my hometown and its people worthy of story—not crime writing or political drama, but stories in which the people take precedence over the institutions. *Lost in the City* is my first love but I'm courting his second collection at the moment because it is newer and sharper and sadder to me. His characters' inner worlds are so richly imagined that I sometimes have trouble making it through the first scene. The words blur to hazy lines and I wonder how it is to live that way, with so many ways of being inside you.

Publius Papinius Statius, *The Thebaid*, translated by Charles Stanley Ross — This is a lesser known classical epic poem loved for its graphic and inventive gore and written off for its discursions and tendency to forgo plot for a tangent. The story is that of the Seven against Thebes, which I believe was first dramatized by Aeschylus. Polynices and Eteocles, sons of Oedipus, fight (epically as you can imagine) for control of the city of Thebes. I have had a dream for years of writing a short story based on one of the many digressions. Hypsipyle recounts a murderous night when the women of Lemnos killed every man and male child. I'm hoping that rereading this will re-inspire me and I'll actually manage to get typing.

Cleanth Brooks and **Robert Penn Warren**, *Understanding Poetry* — I took two poetry classes in college but never enjoyed them. I think I found the brevity of poetry stressful in the same way that movies of substance make me anxious. I feel rushed to parse out every image and allusion in a short span. Novels and television are better for me; there's so much to work with that it's unlikely that you'll ever grasp all there is to see. But a character I'm working on has a more poetic mind than I do. If nothing else, I'm hoping this will introduce me to a good mix of poems. Additionally, if Robert Penn Warren can make me care about southern politics and journalism, he can make poetry manageable.

Posted June 14, 2013.

Martha Nichols

Martha Nichols is editor-in-chief of *Talking Writing*, an online literary magazine and nonprofit organization. A longtime journalist and freelance writer, she has published in *Utne Reader*; *Brain, Child Magazine*; *Youth Today*; *Salon*; and other journals. A former editor at *Harvard Business Review*, she's currently a contributing editor at *Women's Review of Books*. She teaches in the journalism program at the Harvard University Extension School.

Visit her at *Talking Writing*, talkingwriting.com or her website at athenashead.com.

Which pile would you like to hear about? Pinning down the books stacked on and under my nightstand, on the floor beside the shelves near my bed, and on the table next to my favorite reading chair is like capturing a single sequence of thoughts cantering through my mind. Impossible. Hilarious.

But here I am, anyway, attempting an ode to my current state of being. Many of the books in my piles remain unread or partly read. The stack on my nightstand is typical; I've listed the titles below in order, from top to bottom.

The one on the top has spent almost a month there, but oh, how I love the glossy cover: a green vista of a British estate with three foreground figures fashionably dressed in black—two men and a woman in the middle who's holding the hand of the chap on her left, evoking everything and nothing about the story revealed in…

Alan Hollinghurst, *The Stranger's Child* — I just finished this paperback edition of a 2011 novel—and loved it. How have I missed Hollinghurst up to now? A few years ago, I meant to read his Booker-winning *The Line of Beauty*, but it fell off my mental stacks. Now I'll read it, because Hollinghurst is something like a latter-day **E.M. Forster**, one of my very favorite novelists. *The Stranger's Child* is a conscious nod to

Howards End and *Maurice*, especially the latter's exploration of gay relationships in early twentieth-century England. That's a theme in this novel by Hollinghurst, too. But I also thoroughly enjoyed his exploration of the way people's stories shift and change over time—and how attempts to write "The Life" of a well-known poet can founder in a biographer's hands yet brush against larger existential truths.

Dennis Lehane, *Sacred* — A 1997 genre mystery in Lehane's Patrick Kenzie series. In truth, I might have read it way back when, but that didn't stop me from picking up this paperback copy for 50 cents at a school book sale. Sometimes, I just need a good page-turning mystery, and I bet this one is good. *A piece of advice: If you ever follow someone in my neighborhood, don't wear pink.* That opening hooked me. As of two months ago, however, I haven't read past page 6.

David Mitchell, *Cloud Atlas* — The pretty trade paperback edition of this 2004 novel—all those lovely shots of clouds, like something from a meteorologist's commonplace book—has been on my nightstand at various points for years. Every well-intentioned literary reader in my life has insisted that I just *have* to read it. I've never gotten far, but I hauled it out again last fall after seeing the movie of *Cloud Atlas*, which was unexpectedly great and wacky. I figured, "What the heck, don't be a prole, Martha." This time I made it through the first section, which ends in mid-sentence. I hate things that end in mid-sentence. Hollinghurst's novel, which also skips forward in time and between characters, maintains the backbone of a social novel. "Only connect." That's me.

Trevor Corson, *The Secret Life of Lobsters* — Another title I've been meaning to read for ages—this one nonfiction and also originally published in 2004. It documents the "lobstering community" on the Maine island near Acadia National Park where my family and I have summered for a couple of decades. My husband says that a number of the subjects in the book are folks we've met. Still, the blurb on the paperback's front cover—*How Fishermen and Scientists Are Unraveling the Mysteries of Our Favorite Crustacean*—has yet to trap me.

Jane Gardam, *Crusoe's Daughter* — One of a series of novels I've tried this past year that are riffs on classics. (*The Flight of Gemma Hardy* by **Margot Livesey** is another.) I have yet to finish Gardam's erudite spin on novels with faux autobiographical narrators. I'll get back to it, I think. The opening lines of her preface are what convinced me to buy *Crusoe's Daughter*: "This, by far the favourite of all my books, was written thirty years ago after the run of short novels I had rushed off in joyous release but a bit of a sense of sin, the minute the last of my children had gone to school."

Charlotte Brontë, *Jane Eyre* — Here's a genuine classic that I bought in a mass paperback edition in a local Barnes & Noble. As it happened, I'd just read the first chapter of *Gemma Hardy* in the library, not understanding at first that this contemporary novel is a retelling of *Jane Eyre* but thinking, "Huh! Where have I read this scene before?" I connected the dots eventually, and I did finish *Gemma Hardy* on my Kindle—but only after I'd reread most of *Jane Eyre*, which, truly, is tough to improve.

J.R.R. Tolkien, *The Fellowship of the Ring* — I'm reading the series aloud with my son (we finished *The Hobbit* this past summer). Decades ago, it was my *Harry Potter*. Now, my son is taken with the epic tale, although I think the narrative pacing feels like a dawdle for a kid of his generation. Reading it aloud helps. I believe he recognizes the ritual nature of it, too, because we're reading my dad's 1960s paperback edition with the psychedelic cover and yellowed pages that crumble if you handle them too roughly.

Posted January 25, 2013.

Linda Rodriguez

Linda Rodriguez's third Skeet Bannion novel, *Every Hidden Fear*, was published in 2014. Her second Skeet mystery, *Every Broken Trust*, a selection of Las Comadres National Latino Book Club, was a finalist for the Premio Aztlan Literary Prize, and took 2nd Place in the International Latino Book Awards. Her first Skeet novel, *Every Last Secret*, which won the Malice Domestic Best First Traditional Mystery Novel Competition, was a Barnes & Noble mystery pick and a finalist for the International Latino Book Award. Her short story, "The Good Neighbor," which appeared in *Kansas City Noir* (Akashic Books), has been optioned for film.

For her books of poetry, *Skin Hunger* and *Heart's Migration*, Rodriguez received numerous awards and fellowships, including the Midwest Voices and Visions Award, the Thorpe Menn Award, the Elvira Cordero Cisneros Award, and Macondo and Ragdale Fellowships.

She is 2015 Chair of the AWP Indigenous and Aboriginal Writers Caucus, immediate past president of the Borders Crimes chapter of Sisters in Crime, and a member of Wordcraft Circle of Native American Writers and Storytellers, Kansas City Cherokee Community, Latino Writers Collective, The Writers Place, and International Thriller Writers.

Find her on Twitter at twitter.com/rodriguez_linda; on Facebook at facebook.com/LindaRodriguezWrites; and on her own blog, lindarodriguezwrites.blogspot.com, also the *The Stiletto Gang* and *Writers Who Kill* sites. Read an excerpt from her latest at wewantedtobewriters.com/2014/05/excerpt-from-linda-rodriguezs-latest-mystery.

The stack of books by my bed is always teetering. Some of the books are constant residents because I love to reread them or, in the case of anthologies, to dip into them over and over. Some are books I haven't read yet, but have loved earlier books by that author or have had them highly recommended by people whose judgment I trust. Some are advanced reader's copies (ARCs) of books that haven't come out yet that I'm reading for review or to blurb.

Allison Adelle Hedge Coke, editor, *SING: Poetry from the Indigenous Americas* — A marvelous compendium of poems by Indigenous poets from the Arctic Circle to Tierra del Fuego, the first-ever such anthology. Poems are published in the original tribal languages and Spanish, and all are translated into English, as well. The variety of voices is tremendous and the beauty of these poems is breathtaking and lifegiving. I find something to love every time I open this book. Also, editor Hedge Coke has written the great books, *Rock, Ghost, Willow, Deer*, her award-winning memoir; *Dog Road Woman*, her debut collection of poetry that won the American Book Award; and the powerful *Blood Run*, her book of poetry about the moundbuilder Native cultures and the need to preserve the remaining mound complexes from destruction.

Deborah Miranda, *Bad Indians: A Tribal Memoir* — A book I recommend to almost everyone I meet. Miranda has traced the destruction and yet survival of her tribe, the Ohlone-Esselen, as well as other California Indians, through her own ancestors and family, demonstrating the damage done to her tribe and relatives and their immense resilience. This tale has never been told before and is chilling, heartbreaking, and yet full of hope and life.

Joy Castro, *Island of Bones* — This collection of essays was just named a finalist for the PEN/USA Literary Awards in Creative Nonfiction. It takes up where her critically acclaimed memoir, *The Truth Book*, left off. Castro, who was adopted by Cuban-American Jehovah's Witnesses, writes from pain and love with lyrical clarity about gender, identity, violence, class, motherhood, and the academy. She is also the author of two great literary thrillers set in New Orleans, *Hell or High Water* and *Nearer Home*.

Catherine Anderson, *Woman with a Gambling Mania* — Poetry by an award-winning poet, a generous, spirited book, alive and brimming with artists and paintings, crows and rats, portraits of the antique inmates of madhouses and asylums, and the hopeful, desperate lives of immigrants and lovers.

Lorraine López, *The Gifted Gabaldon Sisters* — Another book I often shove into people's hands. A debut novel about four sisters and the ancient servant who raised them and blessed them with gifts at her death, this tour de force is the coming-of-age story of the sisters interwoven with the servant's gripping story of kidnapping and slavery told to a writer long before the girls were born. The book's theme focuses on the lives of women in the past and present, how the distant past informs their present identities, and how they overcome or make peace with the limitations life hands them. This is a book you will go back to again and again. López is also the author of *Homicide Survivors Picnic*, finalist for the prestigious PEN Faulkner Award in Fiction, and *The Realm of Hungry Spirits*, another novel filled with humor and warmth as it details a young Chicana's spiritual journey.

Julia Spencer-Fleming, *One Was a Soldier* — This is simply the best book, fiction or nonfiction, about the toll multiple tours of duty and the corporate corruption of private contractors take on our soldiers in Iraq and Afghanistan and the lack of services we provide for them when they return. All of this is wrapped in a compelling mystery novel, and it's just one of the best books of the past few years. Spencer-Fleming is a gifted novelist with a whole series of impressive mystery novels. I have pre-ordered her newest, forthcoming, *Through the Evil Days*, and am eagerly awaiting its arrival.

Hank Phillippi Ryan, *The Other Woman* — Another favorite mystery novel, this time taking a thoughtful look at ethics in journalism and in politics and the intersection of politics, class, and power in this country. Full of believable characters, fine writing, and complex plot twists, this is a must-read. I've pre-ordered *The Wrong Girl*, the forthcoming sequel.

Posted September 6, 2013.

Linda, continued:

Some of the books by my bed are constant residents because I love to reread them, usually poetry. These books sit with the stacks of books I intend to read because they have been highly recommended by people whose judgment I trust. These are usually novels. The nonfiction books others have recommended or that I'm reading for research sit elsewhere because I like to take notes when reading nonfiction. When I'm sick or stressed, it's poetry to which I turn, however, so I always have some of those favorites at hand.

Walt Whitman, *Leaves of Grass* — This is currently sitting by my bed because I recently took a remarkable MOOC, massive open online course, from the University of Iowa that delved deeply into Whitman's quintessential work in a way that even my graduate work didn't. In this country, *Leaves of Grass* is the bedrock from which most of our best poetry springs, and I find again and again new depths in Whitman's work every time I reread it.

Linda Hogan, *Rounding the Human Corners* — My favorite of Hogan's remarkable books of poetry. It offers visionary imagery and lyrical language, as one had come to expect from Hogan, but the Chickasaw poet is also a dedicated volunteer and consultant for wildlife rehabilitation and endangered species programs and writes with the naturalist's eye and a profound sense of the relationships humans have with the rest of creation, whether we know it or not. Another book I often revisit is Hogan's novel, *Mean Spirit*, which was a finalist for the Pulitzer Award and appears on many lists of Best Novels of the Twentieth Century. This is a stunning and powerful work.

Diane Glancy, *Claiming Breath* — Another of the evergreens that stay on my bedside table. This collection of essays is my favorite among Glancy's many volumes of essays and creative nonfiction. She writes with a poet's eye and ear and with a mystic's sense of the world around her. This Cherokee writer has won so many awards in every genre—poetry, essay/creative nonfiction, short fiction, novel, memoir, stage play, screenplay—that she should hardly need any introduction, yet I'm always amazed at the number of well-read people who are unaware of Glancy's superb work.

Levi Romero, *A Poetry of Remembrance: New and Rejected Works* — A book packed with poems full of powerful emotion, good-natured wit, and a generosity of spirit. Romero takes the reader by the hand and introduces him to the world of families who have been in New Mexico since the Conquistadors and before them. This is a book written with a clear eye, yet it is always apparent how much love for this ancient community of intertwined families informs Romero's work.

Beyond these books, the stack beside my bed varies from week to week, containing ARCs for reviews and blurbs, books others have recommended, and books by authors whose earlier books I've loved. But these books remain from month to month as aids to my meditation and musical delights in which to indulge myself.

Posted May 23, 2014.

James Schwartz

James Schwartz is a poet and slam performer striving for the simplicity of Cavafy mixed with modern gay wordplay and elements. James' poetry/slam material dialogues of GLBTQ issues and affirmations of gay (night) life and love have been published by various poetry journals including *Poetry Life and Times*, *Poetry 24*, *Politiku*, *Babel: The Multilingual Multicultural Online Journal*, *The New Verse News*, *Nostrovia! Poetry,* and *piecejournal*.

His book, *The Literary Party: Growing Up Gay and Amish in America*, was published by inGroup Press in 2011, and new poetry in the anthologies *Among the Leaves: Queer Male Poets on the Midwestern Experience* (2012), and *Milk and Honey* (2013), and the chapbooks, *Alpine Suite* (2013), *Poetry 4 Food 2* (2013), and *Arrival and Departure* (2014).

Visit his website at literaryparty.blogspot.com.

The bookcase beside my bed is Amish made, a hand-crafted remnant of my Amish roots here in Michigan. Browsing a varnished shelf I see both old hardcovers, and a few new. Travel books, poetry collections by C.P. Cavafy and Thom Gunn. No Amish books?

The Old Order Amish have yet to contribute to American literature and letters; although some Amish dabble in religious writing and verse as a hobby and many ex-Amish have written memoirs. An actual career in the Arts would be frowned upon, considered "worldly" and sinful. Considering the drug-addled, booze-drenched legacies of many a poet, they are perhaps justified in this thinking. The Amish Literary Canon as of 2013 would include ex-Amish memoirs, as well as *Boneyard*, by **Stephen Beachy**, the lovely poetry of **Julia Kasdorf** (read her collection of poetry, *Sleeping Preacher*) and my *Literary Party*. **Shelter Somerset** has written several gay Amish romance novels, which is rather fabulous I think!

Few Great American Writers mention the Amish (not even Whitman). John Updike is an exception. I grew up happily without television (and electricity) but my father allowed me free reign at the local library, which fueled my love of (secular) literature and poetry. On winter nights Dad would read aloud from the Bible or chapters from *Robinson Crusoe*.

I spent many days and nights dreaming out my window, dazzled by the great Masters, dizzy from the brilliance of Shakespeare, Whitman, Austen, Shelley, Keats, Byron and Wilde. I longed for literary salons and exotic travels (minus the horse-drawn buggy), to escape the drudgery of my Midwestern Amish existence and onward to **Truman Capote's** *Tangier* or *Ischia*.

I still have my copy of *A Capote Reader* with its gorgeous short stories and European sketches:

> Now that hot weather is here the afternoons are like white midnights; shutters are drawn, sleep stalks the streets (*Ischia*).

> The southern sky was as white and burning as a desert; there was one cloud and it drifted like a traveling oasis (*A Ride Through Spain*).

> From distant towers oboe players serenade before prayers; drums, hidden but heard, tom-tom behind closed doors, and the voices of men, singsonging the Koran, carry out of the mosques into the narrow moon-bright streets (*Tangier*).

I spent a morning in Capote's hometown of Monroeville, Alabama in December 2004, en route to Florida with my father. By now I had read every word Capote published and even Dad had had a good chuckle over *The Grass Harp*. The Faulk House, as Capote's childhood home is called, has burned down but a state marker has been erected and the foundation remains, small pink flowers growing through stone crevices. Dad, being a retired mason, was especially interested, walking the charred perimeter. We take the Monroeville Walking Tour, visit the courthouse where *In Cold Blood* was filmed and dutifully sign the guestbook. The highlight of that crisp, cool day was my Amish Dad striking up a long conversation with a local who just happened to be Harper Lee's mechanic!

Beside *A Capote Reader* is **Hart Crane's** *The Bridge*. Another book I keep returning to. Hart Crane is not an easy read, but patience is a virtue:

> The Morning glory, climbing the morning long Over the lintel on its weary vine, Closes before the dusk, furls in its song As I close mine…

Arthur Rimbaud's masterpiece, *Illuminations*, translated by poet John Ashbery, ever illuminates:

> Graceful son of Pan! Around your forehead crowned with small flowers and berries, your eyes, precious spheres, are moving. (from "Antique")

Next to Rimbaud, on the shelf, are collections of the poetry of **Paul Verlaine**, *Paul Verlaine: Selected Poems*, and **Tomas Transtromer**. Transtromer's *The Great Enigma*, translated by poet Robin Fulton, was the 2011 Nobel Prize Winner in poetry. This collection includes all of Transtromer's brilliant poetry and beautiful prose memoir, *Memories Look At Me.* From his haunting poem "The Crossing-Place":

> Ice-wind in my eyes and the suns dance In the kaleidoscope of tears as I cross The street that's followed me for so long, the street Where Greenland-summer shines from puddles.

Dances for Flute and Thunder: Praises, Prayers, and

Insults, Poems from The Ancient Greek, translated by poet **Brooks Haxton**. This small collection of ancient Greek poetry from 5th century BCE, is a must read. "Three Love Notes" excerpt by Plato:

> When you count the stars, my love, I want to be The night sky, looking into you with all those eyes.

Flesh and Blood by **Michael Cunningham**. Before his brilliant novels *The Hours* and *Specimen Days,* Michael Cunningham wrote this dazzling, epic generation-spanning novel about a Greek immigrant family. Thank me later.

Lastly, *The Great Gatsby* by **F. Scott Fitzgerald**. The new film is fine but it is a film. Read the book if you haven't.

I never imagined I would one day be the first ex-Amish openly gay poet, but it is the reason I keep turning down roles on Amish-esque reality TV. *The literary lights shine brighter than Broadway / Writing until dawn or the kerosene lamp / run too low on oil / to see my dreams.*

Posted June 21, 2013.

Dani Shapiro

Dani Shapiro's most recent books include the memoirs *Devotion* and *Slow Motion*, and the novels *Black & White* and *Family History*. Her stories and essays have appeared in *The New Yorker*, *Granta*, *Tin House*, *One Story*, *Ploughshares*, *Zyzzyva*, and have been broadcast on "This American Life." In 2013 she was Oprah's guest for a one-hour interview on "Super Soul Sunday." She has taught in the creative writing programs at Columbia, NYU, The New School, and Brooklyn College.

You can follow Dani's posts on her website, danishapiro.com; on Facebook at facebook.com/danijshapiro; and Twitter at twitter.com/danijshapiro.

Her newest book, *Still Writing: The Pleasures and Perils of a Creative Life*, is a national bestseller. Read an excerpt at amazon.com/Still-Writing-Pleasures-Perils-Creative/dp/0802121403.

The books I'm either reading, or want to be reading, or should be reading, exist in a constant state of migration between the bookcase in my office, my office floor, and the chaise longue in my office. Sometimes I give up, and slink down the stairs to my library, and shelve the book, realizing that I'm not going to get to it. Not now. Perhaps not ever. But when a book makes it to my nightstand, it doesn't leave my nightstand until I have read it. Therefore, I have a teetering pile on my nightstand. If that pile fell over in the middle of the night, it would wake up the whole household.

A few of these books are mainstays. I've read them more than once. I dip in and out of them. The first of these is **Jack Kornfield**'s *A Path With Heart: A Guide Through the Perils and Promises of Spiritual Life*, a wise and beautifully written guide to a contemplative life. I've gotten to know Jack a little over the past few years, and I can hear his voice as I read him.

The same goes for **Sylvia Boorstein**, another great

Buddhist thinker and writer, and a very dear friend, whose books spoke to me long before I knew her. *Happiness is an Inside Job* stays on my nightstand, a way of keeping her close.

The writer and neuroscientist **David Eagleman**'s brilliant little book, *Sum: Forty Tales from the Afterlives*, manages to be both poetry and philosophy, at once magical and grounded. These brief tales also have the benefit of being very short. A perfect bit of reading before bed. I try to fall asleep with good sentences in my ears. In this category I would also put **Annie Dillard**'s *The Writing Life*, which is hands-down my favorite book on writing, and one that I have kept near me at all times while working on my own book on writing. It's not a craft book, not instructive in any practical way, but contains such wisdom and thoughtfulness about what it takes to live the life of a writer.

Until recently, **Meg Wolitzer**'s *The Interestings* had a place on my nightstand, but I tore through it in just a couple of weeks—such was her mastery of character and story and the movement of time—and since I finished it, now the big fat novel on my nightstand is *& Sons* by **David Gilbert**, which I'm very much enjoying.

And I always have a few recent issues of *One Story*, the literary magazine that contains one single gem of a story in each issue. They've just excerpted a piece of **Elizabeth Gilbert**'s new novel, *The Signature of All Things*. That's what's next.

Posted September 20, 2013.

Kitty Sheehan

Kitty Sheehan is a writer, photographer and founder/director of the Dartbrook Writers Retreat in Keene, NY. A native Iowan and graduate of the University of Iowa, Kitty taught elementary school in Minneapolis, was a corporate trainer, a graphic designer, a consignment store owner and a social media editor. Her resume's a riot. After a bucolic interlude residing in New York's Hudson Valley, she's back in Minnesota for now. Her essays have appeared in Hudson Valley magazine, online in Drinking Diaries and various other places around the web.

Visit her website at kittysheehan.com or follow her on Twitter at twitter.com/KittyASheehan. Or find out more about Dartbrook at dartbrookwriters.com.

The pile of books by my bed gets unruly and begins to mock me when I've been spending too much time online and not holding and reading a real book. I'll see it then as if for the first time. "Oh, hey, what's this?" Here's what's waiting for me now:

Mary Cantwell, *Manhattan Memoir* — This is actually three books in one. Mary Cantwell first chronicled her New England girlhood in *American Girl*, and went on to write two more books, *Manhattan, When I Was Young*, about her career in New York's magazine scene in the 1950s, and finally *Speaking with Strangers*, which finds her a single mother struggling to make her way in her beloved city. The three combined are under 500 pages.

I love New York, I love magazines, and I love memoir, so this book is a comfortable breeze through a life that's never dull. Cantwell's writing style is clean and honest; she needs no tricks to get across her sometimes funny, sometimes sad and confused voice. It's *The Devil Wears Prada* meets "Mad Men," but not wrapped in a bright shiny marketing package—just wrapped in wonderful writing. After working at *Mademoiselle* in the 50s, Cantwell went on to write a *New York Times* column for women in the '80s. Remember the '80s? Remember women in the '80s? Check her out.

And now for something completely different:

Neil Young, *Waging Heavy Peace* — I'm a little afraid of this one. I can tell it's going to be just like a Neil Young song, or a Neil Young interview—a puzzle that leaves you completely entranced and awed when you finally figure it out. I consider him nothing short of a genius. So I'm ready to dive in, prepared to be suspended in his mesmerizing world for a while. Here's an excerpt, which is the only writing on the front jacket flap:

> I think I will have to use my time wisely and keep my thoughts straight if I am to succeed and deliver the cargo I so carefully have carried thus far to the outer reaches. Not that it's my only job or task. I have others, too. Sacred things that I need to protect from pain and hardship, like careless remarks on an open mind.

See what I mean?

Speaking of puzzles, are you one of those habitual obituary readers? I am. I occasionally get to write them too, which gives me great appreciation for those who've mastered the art.

Marilyn Johnson, *The Dead Beat: Lost Souls, Lucky Stiffs, and the Perverse Pleasures of Obituaries* — This is the golden ticket for the obit-aholic. Johnson, an obituary writer herself, takes us deep inside what she does. She's funny, she's smart, she's ultra-observant and she's a great writer.

She details how editors and obit writers thrill to the kinds of coincidences that put two Medal of Honor winners from two eras side by side on the same day's obituary page. We meet the subjects of obits as well as the writers of some of her favorite obits. She lets us in on the thought processes that brought forth her classic tribute to Marlon Brando when he died at age 80.

She's masterful at pulling out the details that make a person's life vivid, unique and meaningful to those of us left behind to read and remember. Johnson engagingly writes in first person about her joyous and productive obsession with obits from around the world. You'll have new appreciation for the details that make us human, and the ones that make for a good story. This book is a jewel.

And here's the one that's always in the pile, the one that never leaves:

Abigail Thomas, *A Three Dog Life* — Abby's my teacher and my friend. I love her and her writing. You will too, I promise, if you read this: her memoir of losing her husband in a car accident. He didn't die; he suffered severe brain damage. He lost all memory.

Abby is one of the strongest, funniest and brave people you'll ever meet, and it's all here. To be in her presence is to watch her make something from nothing, over and over— whether it's with words, food, paint or treasures from the junk shop. She builds things. This book is about how she built a new life after a surreal tragedy stole the one she had. It's also a memoir anchored in love and rebirth.

Also in my current stack are a Joan Didion and a Nora Ephron. Isn't that the rule?

Posted October 12, 2012.

Trip Starkey

Trip Starkey is currently a Graduate Teaching Fellow and MFA student at The University of Oregon. He received a bachelor's degree in English Literature from Texas Christian University. He spends most of his time writing poetry, essays, and book reviews. He also helps with the Lit Blogging at *The Literary Man*.

Visit his website at tripstarkey.com.

As you can assume, the organizational skills of any 21-year-old college male are rarely up to the standards of normal, self-sustained adults. So as to not disappoint my mother, I have made it my utmost priority to neatly organize, stack, and shelve the hundreds of books in my apartment. A task that, at times, seems to be more than I can handle. This often results in mounds of books being sporadically placed across my floor.

When I began taking my studies seriously as a sophomore in college (arriving one year late to the party), I also began acquiring books somewhat frequently. Taking on the task of reviewing books for a blog only seemed to perpetuate my problem of acquisition. Now, entering my senior year of college, I have come to find myself walled in by books, praying each day that a fire does not break out.

Scanning the towers of books on the floor next to my bed, I see some great titles that have served (and are continuing to serve) as guides to my own understanding of the world.

Note: I have a quirk. I tend to keep stacks with multiple genres near my bed, giving myself a variety of styles to choose from when I read. (Or, in other words, I don't take care to arrange by any particular method).

The fiction I have favored lately includes the wonderfully brilliant novel *Gilead* by **Marilynne Robinson**, and the hell-spun short-story collection *I Hate To See That Evening Sun Go Down* by **William Gay**. Robinson provides me with the spiritual guidance needed by any young person (religious or not), while Gay provides wildly entertaining gothic tales that never fail to disturb the peacefulness of sleep.

For nonfiction I have **Kevin Young's** artfully crafted *The Grey Album: On The Blackness of Blackness*, which is a stunning delve into African American culture. It is a skillfully written study by one of my favorite working writers. I also have **Zora Neale Hurston's** memoir *Dust Tracks on a Road*, which is a charming chronicle of her life as a storyteller growing up in the segregated, rural south.

As for poetry, I have been working my way through **Frank Stanford's** haunting epic *The Battlefield Where The Moon Says I Love You*. This 15,000-line poem is one of the most intriguing works I've read in the American canon. Written entirely without punctuation, it requires all brain function, and completely engrosses you as a reader. The other collection I have been ingesting is *Bye-and-Bye: Selected Late Poems* by **Charles Wright**. A brilliant poet, Wright has been able to focus me as a young writer, helping me along with vibrant imagery and a fervent message.

Finally, I have a few light reads for entertainment. The first one is *Who Killed John F. Kennedy* by the ever-hilarious guys over at **Despair, Inc**. The book takes the form of a Choose Your Own Adventure story, a favorite for children of the '80s and '90s. However, this detective story is rigged. It can only end in defeat. I have found myself laughing out loud on multiple occasions, and the book is very well made with great illustrations and plot. The other entertaining reading I have next to my bed is *The Habit of Being: Letters of Flannery O'Connor* (selected and edited by Sally Fitzgerald. This collection of letters by one of my all-time favorite authors opens the door to all facets of **Flannery O'Connor's** personality, and is a truly delightful read.

These books, along with others, make up the accumulation next to my bed, and each of them garnishes an ecstatic recommendation from me.

Posted August 9, 2013.

Ann Elia Stewart

Ann Elia Stewart is the author of *Twice a Child*, a story of love, loss and forgiveness. The main character, an elderly man in the early stages of Lewy Body Dementia, embarks upon a cross-country journey to find his estranged son. In 2010, Stewart's own father succumbed to LBD, a rare form of dementia that combines both Alzheimer's and Parkinson's Disease.

She calls her debut novel a "love letter" to her father. She earned a fellowship in fiction from the Pennsylvania Council on the Arts, and has enjoyed an extensive career in all facets of writing, including journalism, advertising copywriting, and creative nonfiction. Stewart facilitates a popular creative writing workshop for the Fredricksen Library in Camp Hill, Pennsylvania. She edited the first anthology of short stories generated from that workshop, entitled *A Community of Writers*. She also teaches creative writing at the Capital Area School for the Arts Charter School in Harrisburg, Pennsylvania.

Read more about Ann and her books at tbrtheblog.blogspot.com/2012/06/tbr-welcomes-ann-elia-stewart.html.

I am a nibble reader. I usually have several books going at a time, as well as magazine articles or articles I have downloaded to be read in the comfort of my bed. So here is a sample of what I've been nibbling.

Aimee Bender, *The Particular Sadness of Lemon Cake* — Bender's analogies are like petit fours: so beautiful you are compelled to pick them up or, in my case, write them down and admire their exquisite quirks. Here's one: Her protagonist is nine-year-old Rose who can taste emotion in food, as well as pinpoint its origin. She says of a friend who has consumed a bowl of oatmeal prepared by a faceless character named Janet:

"Without tasting even a speck of hurry in Janet's oatmeal, which was so rushed it was like eating the calendar of an executive's. . ." Or of a chocolate chip cookie she sensed was made in anger: "The whole cookie was so rushed like I had to eat it fast or it would, somehow, eat me." The novel provides a unique look into a dysfunctional family as told through Rose; it could almost pass for a memoir.

Gary Chapman, *The 5 Love Languages* — Sometimes long-term unions deserve tune-ups. This book brings troubled couples together, sparks conversation that pushes aside argument and allows for the reason you came together in the first place. It illuminates the art of conversation that can be verbal or silent. And it helps couples struggling to find a voice amid the chaos of living by homing in on each member's unique need to be heard. It's fun to guess your partner's love language, but even better, it's fulfilling to watch a relationship bloom again when you take to heart the advice contained within this precious little book.

Anne Tyler, *The Accidental Tourist* — I rotate beloved books. Last year's included **Fitzgerald's** *The Great Gatsby* (nine perfect chapters). This year it's Anne Tyler's classic tale of mourning as told through her signature complex and quirky characters, Macon and Muriel. I cry all over again and I renew the drive to write all over again: Make me laugh, make me cry. Make me FEEL.

Stacy Schiff, *Cleopatra: A Life* — This is a book I pick up and read a page or so at a time to savor the rich words of painstaking research: details that allow the reader to step into Cleopatra's skin as she discovers the crudities and oddities of a city called Rome, far different from her beloved Alexandria. Witness: "If she spent any time in the thick of the city, Cleopatra found herself amid a gloomy welter of crooked, congested streets... among muddy pigs and soup vendors and artisans' shops that tumbled out onto footways. By every measure a less salubrious city than Alexandria, Rome was squalid and shapeless, an oriental tangle of narrow, poorly ventilated streets and ceaseless, shutter-creaking commotion, perpetually in shadow, stiflingly hot in summer." Whether I want to be or not — I'm there!

And the book I will read after I am through *Lemon Cake*:

Jennie Fields, *The Age of Desire* — I love books told from various points of view. My own book is constructed in this way. I am intrigued by and highly anticipate the perspectives of Edith Wharton and her literary secretary and confidante, Anna Bahlmann. The novel comes highly recommended by a friend, herself a voracious reader.

Passed on to another reader, but an honorary book-by-the-bed:

Sarah Waters, *Fingersmith* — Waters takes a stab at a Dickensian world of orphanages, thievery, and veiled pornography. I was immediately transported to the filthy and ribald living of late nineteenth century England where a tale of two points of view at once intrigue and befuddle, daring you to read between the lines as one of Waters' two heroines reads "tales" to an audience of elderly gents from her "uncle's" vast collection of precious and rare books. It's worth noting that I read this as I was giving *Fifty Shades of Grey* a go (curious as to how such a book could garner millions of readers and dollars). While the latter lasted three chapters before I threw it across the room, *Fingersmith's* sly hints of sexual longing as well as mental gymnastics for what is not being said kept me turning the pages in fervor.

Posted October 5, 2012.

Susan Tepper

Susan Tepper is the author of four published books of fiction and a chapbook of poetry. *The Merrill Diaries* is a novel in stories that begins in 1976 and follows a 21-year-old Merrill for a decade, over two continents and multitudinous adventures involving hit men, hookers, psychics, love, lust, and the music business. Tepper shares a Pulitzer Prize nomination (with co-author Gary Percesepe) for their epistolary novel *What May Have Been: Letters of Jackson Pollock & Dori G*. Additionally she has received nine Pushcart Prize nominations. Her story "Distance" is on the notable stories list for *storySouth* Million Writers Award, 2014. Tepper is a contributing editor at *Flash Fiction Chronicles* where she conducts the author/book interview series UNCOV/rd. She also writes a monthly column about all things literary called "Let's Talk" at *Black Heart Magazine*. FIZZ, her reading series at KGB Bar in NYC, has been ongoing sporadically for seven years.

Visit her website at susantepper.com.

Because my writer brain is on even-split mode between fiction and poetry, I have a pile of both on my hammered-tin bed table from Morocco (purchased at HomeGoods, as I'm still waiting to get to Morocco). I also have books on the floor, on my dresser, and on a green wicker chair near the window.

Simon Perchik, *Hands Collected: The Books of Simon Perchik Poems: 1949 – 1999* — This is Perchik's opus that will stay with me 'til my croaking end, which could be soon at the rate things are going. Just kidding, though there are a few contracts out on me (not two book deals either)! Perchik is my poet of choice, hands down, hands collected, hands clapping. He gets into the soul-soil in every poem and just annihilates me. I also have his brand new book *Almost Rain* which sits nicely on top of *Hands Collected*. As if the hands are holding the rain.

William Trevor, *The Collected Stories* — Taught me how to write fiction. Though we are thematically different, I learned about clean writing and truth from Trevor's work, that each story must tell some profound truth if the protagonist and supporting cast are to come alive on the page. Trevor never fails me.

Jerome Loving, *Walt Whitman: The Song of Himself* — A biography that keeps my poet faith alive. I grew up just a mile or so from the Walt Whitman House in Huntington, Long Island. My mom used to take us on walks past his house to buy candy from a tiny local farm stand kind of store. She would say, "That's where the famous poet Walt Whitman used to live." It was all so beautifully overgrown and peeling paint back then, before the restorers stepped in. I've been reading this biography slowly, for a decade now. It is long at 568 pages. But I think I don't want it to end.

Mark Helprin, *Memoir from Antproof Case* — This novel is another book I've been reading for a long time. I have it in hardcover, first printing, and the book is this beautiful thing made to look like rough beige texture (an antproof case) and tied both ways in mock-string. I have a deep feeling for the story and for the book itself. I also like boxes and cases a lot, and this book exemplifies all that. Plus it's a hell of a good tale.

James Baldwin, *Another Country* — Utterly slayed me. I received it as a gift from Eric Darton this past winter, for no reason other than he felt I should read it. I milked it into spring, that's how badly I didn't want this novel to end. Now I'm going to read Baldwin's entire canon of literature.

So here you have my split brain offering up half fiction and half poetry. Many more books reside at my bedside, but these are the books I'd like to share right now.

Posted November 15, 2013.

Tom Titus

Dr. Tom A. Titus is author of the memoir *Blackberries in July: A Forager's Field Guide to Inner Peace*, a year-long chronology of old orchards, bay clams, wild mushrooms, and spawning salmon, a hunting and gathering of his spirit that became a reunion with the land and family traditions.

Tom owes his existence to three generations of ancestors who lived in the wet green creases of the Oregon Coast Range. He was raised in the Willamette Valley foothills near Eugene on an outdoor diet of fishing, hunting, backpacking, and mountaineering.

His taste for foraging and far-flung places led to a BA in biology at Western Oregon State University. He left his natal Pacific Northwest to attend the University of Kansas, where he completed a PhD in evolutionary genetics. Tom returned to Oregon in 1994, where he is a research biologist and instructor at the University of Oregon. In his spare time he is a writer, runner, gardener, husband, father of two, and seeker of wild things and the wise quiet spaces in which they are found.

Follow Tom on Facebook at facebook.com/tom.titus.9400; read an excerpt from his book at wewantedtobewriters.com/2013/03/excerpt-from-tom-titus-memoir.

I am an insomniac.

One would think that in those hours without sleep the books by my bed would be consumed like dry kindling in a hot fire. But this is not my lot in literary life, because I can fall asleep in five breaths without reading a word. Yet I choose to read, even though this often requires an act of will that could entail five words or five paragraphs or on a big night five pages. Sleeplessness comes five hours later when I turn like a turkey on a slow rotisserie, sometimes writing poetry in my head, other times wrestling with the great questions of the universe such as whether to have a fried egg and toast or oatmeal before going to a job that I love but not as much as I love writing but I go to anyway because while writing covers my karmic debt to all things, being a research geneticist pays the mortgage. So be it.

Sharing these intimate details of my nightlife is a roundabout explanation for why books by my bed are more akin to damp logs on a cold fire. They have staying power. They pile up. While I've never before stepped back to examine the literary heap on my small white nightstand *in toto*, from a distance I see that the volumes accumulating there do have some things in common. They are nearly all poetry, essay collections, and other nonfiction that can be read in the short space of consciousness preceding that dark inexorable wave that sweeps it all away. My books are various explorations into the idea of Place, that little spot in the universe to which we have attached ourselves and connect with on all levels. I believe in Place and am committed to the idea that we become whole people when we are physically, emotionally, and spiritually connected to our world. I am fascinated by authors who effectively communicate this relationship through science or art or personal experience or some unified connection among all of these.

Aldo Leopold, *A Sand County Almanac* — The *Almanac* is first on my list because of its broad importance to modern conservationists and its influence on my personal philosophy. I have read this book cover to cover at least twice, and it remains on my nightstand where I occasionally grab it for random explorations into Leopold's thinking on connectedness. What do I love about Aldo Leopold? He engaged with the land on multiple levels; he was a forester, a hunter, a fisherman, a preservationist, and an academic, all encapsulated into an environmental philosopher who saw that humans become fully actualized when they are engaged with the land. Leopold put this ethic into practice by investing in the ecological recovery of a small run-down farm in Saulk County, Wisconsin. The *Almanac* is a seasonal chronology of essays around the farm followed by other writings that culminate in his essay "The Land Ethic," in which he challenges us to extend our concept of morality beyond human-human interactions to human interactions with the land. What fascinates me as much as the conservationist philosophy embodied in Leopold's writings is his transformation as a writer. There is little doubt that his philosophy evolved along with his voice, which speaks to the introspective nature of the art. I love this book.

Robert Michael Pyle, *The Tangled Bank* — This collection of essays was written during Pyle's ten-year tenure as a columnist for *Orion* magazine. His all-encompassing grasp of the natural world is nearly daunting, and the compact prose with which he communicates this knowledge is impressive. Pyle begins by proclaiming, "There's barely a place, scarcely a square inch with any visible life or color to it that can't catch and keep my interest, at least for a spell." Fifty-two essays later I am convinced. My favorites are "Losers Keepers," in which he confesses to being a loser of things (I have discovered a kindred spirit!), and "Hanky Panky: Notes on the Biology of Boogers," a treatise on the finer points of snot written when he had a killer cold. One thousand words each; the perfect length for an unlikely insomniac-naturalist capable of falling asleep almost immediately.

Robin Wall Kimmerer, *Gathering Moss* — These wonderful essays were written by a member of the Potawatomi Tribe who is a PhD bryologist (moss biologist) and Professor of Environmental Biology at the State University of New York College of Environmental Science and Forestry. In her exploration of the magical world of mosses, Dr. Kimmerer moves seamlessly between the perspectives of "western" scientific thinking and the spiritual/ecological traditions of her Native American heritage. Her book has given me new ways to view the land: how to really *see* the diminutive mosses and their impact on the landscape and a philosophy that integrates the findings of western biology with traditional ecological knowledge and spiritual connections to our Place. Robin's new book is *Braiding Sweetgrass*. Don't miss it!

Kathryn Ridall, *What the River Brings: Oregon River Poems* — At a recent William Stafford poetry reading I found myself deep in conversation with Kathryn about the meaning of place for a fourth generation Oregonian like myself compared with her two years of experience here. Kathryn anchored herself in Eugene by immediately developing an intimate connection with the Willamette River. She has written poetry around the river, gathered the poems of other western river poets, and produced this collection. These poems sing with the liquid voice of moving water, the rattle of sunlit riffles splashing into clear pools where salmon rest and water and time and thinking move deeply. This is music to fall asleep by.

John Daniel, *Of Earth* — John Daniel knows the music of words and was a contributor to *What the River Brings*. Although he is renown for his prose, especially memoirs such as *Rogue River Journal* and *Winter Creek*, John was a Wallace Stegner Fellow in Poetry and has produced an impressive body of verse over his decades of writing in the West. His poems remind me that people are a part of nature, that we can go out, reach out, and draw ourselves into the living world. John's poetry is fluid, unassuming, unpretentious, completely accessible, and at the end of the evening will draw you in without a struggle.

Tim Whitsel, *We Say Ourselves* — When I was nineteen all I wanted in life was to play jazz trombone. I ended up a biologist. But Tim Whitsel's poetry reminds me of that old dream; the sometimes syncopation, the ebb and flow and rise and fall of rhythm in his words, the interwoven images of my native McKenzie River Valley and people living their flawed meaningful lives. What I *really* love is watching and listening to Tim read his stuff; he loves jazz, too, and it shows. But on most evenings I'll settle for "How I See You Canning Tomatoes" just before switching off the light. Magic.

Posted March 2, 2013.

Lee Upton

Lee Upton is the author of *The Tao of Humiliation: Stories*, which was released from BOA Editions in 2014. She has also written 12 other books, including the essay collection *Swallowing the Sea: On Writing & Ambition, Boredom, Purity & Secrecy*; the novella *The Guide to the Flying Island*; and a fifth collection of poetry, *Undid in the Land of Undone*. She is a professor of English and the writer-in-residence at Lafayette College.

Visit her website at sites.lafayette.edu/uptonlee. Read an excerpt from her latest at wewantedtobewriters.com/2014/05/excerpt-from-lee-uptons-new-book.

I have to confess that my bedside reading is not like the other reading I do in other parts of the house. The reason is simple: I am a susceptible reader right before bed, when I feel most porous and undefended. And so the books by my bed have, for the most part, a peculiar quality—they tend to be more otherworldly and dreamlike than other books I enjoy, and less often marked by overt or unrelenting violence or violence that isn't somehow mediated.

Correction:

Having made the above declaration, I realize that the book in nearest finger-reach beside my bed is **Julio Cortázar**'s *Blow-Up and Other Stories,* which includes "Night Face Up" with its no-holds-barred portrayal of human sacrifice—so far my favorite story in the collection, a wild story in which dream life and so-called actual life are interchanged. And in which a man on a stone slab is about to get his heart ripped out.

Rebecca Mead, *My Life in Middlemarch* — Mead uses George Eliot's novel to think about her own life—and uses her own life to think about the novel. The result is intimate and yet probing. Sometimes you feel like you're reading gorgeous, high-end gossip about Eliot's characters and Eliot herself.

But you can read it guiltlessly; no reputations will have been harmed in the making of this book.

Robin Robertson, *Slow Air* — This collection by the Scottish poet is characterized by restraint. I've read these evocative poems repeatedly, with awe at the ways in which Robertson's lines about elemental matters—nature and love—expand in the mind and resonate.

Iris Murdoch, *The Sea, The Sea* — I keep this novel about an obsessive, controlling, and arrogant retired actor/director near my bed to dip into. Here's a passage I've marked in red: "Even in a harmless fall in the road there is a little moment of horror when the faller realizes that he *cannot help himself*; he has been taken over by a relentless mechanism and must continue with it to the end and be subject to the consequences."

Murdoch can take a moment and extend it, as if she's putting us all in training to notice things we otherwise would ignore. She shows how we can keep falling in many ways—and realize we're falling while we're falling, which is one of the worst parts of falling. Her descriptions of the sea are breath-taking, and I'm not exaggerating.

George Schenk, *Moss Gardening: Including Lichens, Liverworts, and Other Miniatures* — A charming book with plentiful photographs of moss and other small entities. Here's a sample of the author's characteristic blend of pride and self-deprecation as he describes his purpose: "[This book] tells almost as much about the mechanics of moss gardening as the Kama Sutra does about dancing. Like that book, this work of mine may offer more variations on the theme than you really care to know."

It's nice to have this eccentric and pure labor of love nearby, not only for its images but for the author's appealing voice. I haven't finished the book, but it doesn't seem as if it requires finishing.

Lydia Davis, *Can't and Won't: Stories* — Davis's stories are almost always very short, and yet they behave with such large-scale authority. Her narrators look around themselves with an air of low-key amusement or quiet astonishment. At other times Davis allows her narrators to make soft landings on near-revelations.

Janet Burroway, editor, *A Story Larger Than My Own: Women Writers Look Back on Their Lives and Careers* — Included are essays by nineteen writers, among them, **Margaret Atwood**, **Gail Godwin**, **Honor Moore**, **Jane Smiley**, and **Edith Pearlman**. The latter notes: "To respond positively to an invitation to Appear in Public is the acme of masochism."

Nice little bonus: It's a handsome book, with an old-style image of a library card pocket on the cover. Before I open the book I spend a moment enjoying that cover. I haven't read the entire collection yet. I've been so busy with that cover.

Edward St. Aubyn, *The Patrick Melrose Novels*: *Never Mind, Bad News, Some Hope, and Mother's Milk* — Terrors are contained in each of the four slim novels in this collection—and so much vulnerability. The plots are harrowing, and yet the prose in its precision is somehow redemptive. St. Aubyn creates sealed worlds of incredible privilege where adult pathologies, boredom, and frustration are accompanied by cruelty toward the most vulnerable, cruelty that seems renewable. And yet the books, balanced between bleak tragedy and bitterly comic malice, are beautiful—as if description itself is the best revenge.

Posted May 30, 2014.

Suzy Vitello

As a founding member of what *The Oregonian* has dubbed Portland's "hottest writing group" (members include Chuck Palahniuk, Chelsea Cain, Lidia Yuknavitch, Monica Drake, and Cheryl Strayed), Suzy Vitello's name has graced the acknowledgement pages of many a book.

Her own award-winning writing has appeared in *Mississippi Review*, *Plazm*, and other journals. *Unkiss Me*, an e-chapbook of her stories is available at your favorite online retailer. She holds an MFA from Antioch Los Angeles, and when she's not writing novels, she does freelance copywriting, editing and teaching. *The Moment Before* is her debut novel, and a second novel, *The Empress Chronicles*, was released this year. Suzy lives in Portland, Oregon with her husband Kirk, and son Carson.

Find out more about Suzy on her website, suzyvitello.com.

I've just devoured a couple of newer books, and revisited another collection of long-standing in preparation for a class I'm teaching.

By "devoured" I mean chewed and swallowed carefully. Slowly. I'm not a speedy reader, and, in fact, long to linger with the books I love. As I approach the final 50 pages of a beloved story, I tend to get melancholy. It's a sort of grief that sets in. That was particularly my experience with **Tom Spanbauer**'s new novel, *I Loved You More*.

ILYM is a story about a man who loves another man, and the woman who fucks that all up. It's billed as a "love triangle" but that's just marketing speak, I think. What drives this particular story is the intensity of love experienced by the first person narrator, Ben.

Ben, a gay man whose depth of humanity has driven him into the arms of women as well, falls for a straight guy, Hank, whom he meets in a NYC writing class. Hank is the star of the prestigious writing class, so, as in most classic love stories, the beginning of the relationship is rocky, in that "meet cute" way. But soon, Ben is smitten, and the two fellows develop a bosom buddy secret language. Only, for Ben, it goes beyond platonic.

Hank is volatile, full of shame, and uses his bottomless supply of charisma to move through the world in what appears to be compensation for his deep doubts about himself.

The novel spans decades, and through most of the chronology Hank and Ben do not live in the same town, but Hank occasionally appears prodigal-like for comfort, which Ben offers and offers again.

Then, Ben has a health crisis and practically dies. That's when one of his students, Ruth, swoops in and saves—and then slowly takes over—his life.

Eventually things go awry between Ben and Ruth, and, coincidentally, that's when Hank pays a visit.

Spanbauer's lyric, visceral, precise language is prose poetry on the page. His unflinching voice, his willingness to look at the truth even when the truth ain't pretty—that's what makes his work unique and intimate. This is a book you'll need two of. One to keep, and one to loan.

And while we're on the subject of books you might want a couple of, have you read **Jess Walter**'s *Beautiful Ruins*? I admit, I'm late to the Jess Walter party, but I'm catching up. In this novel, his sixth, Walter has a big story to tell. One with popular culture historical details: Liz and Dick on the Cleopatra set in the '60s. Told third person from several points of view, *Beautiful Ruins*, like the Spanbauer book, spans decades. The chapters seem disparate at first, but quickly build cohesion, and dovetail to produce an engrossing, hilarious and heart-breaking story.

This book marries wit, history, yearning, the shallowness of popular culture, and the passion and drive to live a valuable life. It's all there, and it's another one that filled me with grief when I finished it.

So those are a couple of newer books. But a classic that is

never far from my reach is **Flannery O'Connor**'s *Complete Stories*, (originally published 1971 by Farrar, Straus and Giroux). When I need a tune-up in precision and clarity (as a writer), I leaf through O'Connor, and I'll get what I'm after. Take, for instance, the way she begins *A Good Man is Hard to Find*, one of her signature stories:

> The grandmother didn't want to go to Florida. She wanted to visit some of her connections in east Tennessee and she was seizing at every chance to change Bailey's mind. Bailey was the son she lived with, her only boy. He was sitting on the edge of his chair at the table, bent over the orange sports section of the Journal. "Now look here, Bailey," she said, "see here, read this," and she stood with one hand on her thin hip and the other rattling the newspaper at his bald head. "Here this fellow that calls himself The Misfit is aloose from the Federal Pen and headed toward Florida and you read here what it says he did to these people. Just you read it. I wouldn't take my children in any direction with a criminal like that aloose in it. I couldn't answer to my conscience if I did."

With that opening, we have conflict, action, personality, intent. We have physical business, the promise of a plot. Great, precise attention to language and scene setting. Before I sit down with my own pages (i.e. blank computer screen), I often read a bit of O'Connor. It's like stretching before a race: loosens the writing muscle, takes me away from the normative world of monkey-mind, and opens me up to my own tentative imagination.

And, speaking of writing, I'd better snap to it! I'm deep into my *The Moment Before* sequel, and I can't stand to be away from my characters too long!

Posted April 11, 2014.

JC Wall

Judy Clement Wall's short stories, essays, reviews and interviews have been published in numerous literary print journals and on websites such as *The Rumpus*, *Huffington Post*, *Lifebyme*, *Smith Magazine*, *Used Furniture Review*, *Beyond The Margins*, and *Clamp*.

You can read more of her work and engage in her shenanigans on her website, judyclementwall.com.

On my nightstand there are nine books. Three of them I'm reading now…

Cheryl Strayed, *Tiny Beautiful Things* — A collection of online advice columns for the literary website, *The Rumpus*. I've been a Dear Sugar (and Cheryl Strayed) fan for a long time, so I've already read most of the sad, heroic, wrenching, inspiring, edgy, outrageous, ordinary, beautiful letters in this collection. I'm reading them again now because, honestly, I find our shared human frailty and our willingness to love each other in spite of all the reasons not to ridiculously reassuring. Plus, no one writes naked, brave and straight-from-the-heart like Sugar.

Brené Brown, *Daring Greatly: How the Courage to Be Vulnerable Transforms the Way We Live, Love, Parent, and Lead* — The shame researcher's latest. I've been a Brené Brown follower since April of 2010, when I watched her TED Talk, "The Power of Vulnerability." In that talk, she said people who have a strong sense of love and belonging are people who believe that what makes them vulnerable, makes them beautiful. It was exactly what I needed to hear when I needed to hear it. *Daring Greatly* takes its title from a Teddy Rooselvelt quote, which is just too excellent not to share:

> It is not the critic who counts; not the man who points

> out how the strong man stumbles, or where the doer of deeds could have done them better. The credit belongs to the man who is actually in the arena, whose face is marred by dust and sweat and blood; who strives valiantly; who errs, who comes up short again and again, because there is no effort without error and shortcoming; but who does actually strive to do the deeds; who knows great enthusiasms, the great devotions; who spends himself in a worthy cause; who at the best knows in the end the triumph of high achievement, and who at the worst, if he fails, at least fails while daring greatly.

Joyce Carol Oates, *Them* — The first novel I've ever read by her. I admitted online never having read a JCO novel (only her short stories) and a friend who had just cleaned out the back office of the literary journal where she works, sent me this book she'd found there. (Say what you will about how Facebook is making us lonelier, but magic like that happens too.) *Them* is gritty and sad and strangely mesmerizing; I'm about 65 pages from being done and I'm liking it quite a bit. It won't be my last JCO novel.

There are also three books by my bed that I've already read…

Anne Lamott, *Bird by Bird: Some Instructions on Writing and Life* — This is the writing book that follows me wherever I go. I keep it close by because it soothes my troubled writer's soul. I reread passages all the time. My copy of the book opens automatically to "shitty first drafts," which I can practically recite.

David Rakoff, *Half Empty* — I love this collection of essays that spears everything from healthcare to pop culture to literature to technology. Critics, when they review Rakoff's essay collections, often focus on his pessimism and his biting, sharp wit, but underneath that is the thing that draws me to his work again and again: a defiant sort of sweetness, an underlying hope. I read *Half Empty* just before I went to see This American Life's live show, in which Rakoff read and danced (and broke my heart). Shortly after that show, he became yet another amazing voice silenced by cancer. I keep his book out because cancer just plain pisses me off… and I guess I want to stay mad.

Aimee Bender, *Willful Creatures* — Recently, I wrote a blog post about how tricky language can be. I used the term "motherfucker" to make a point, and that started a conversation on Twitter about Aimee Bender's wonderful short story, "Motherfucker." The Twitter exchange made me want to read the story again, and the story made me want to read the whole collection again, and so there it is. *Willful Creatures*. By my bed.

The last three books on my nightstand, I haven't read yet, but one of them will be next. They are *The Story of a Marriage* by **Andrew Sean Greer**; *The Hunger Games* by **Suzanne Collins**; and *Two Girls, Fat and Thin* by **Mary Gaitskill**.

If you want to vote on what I tackle next, feel free. (You can even suggest something not currently by my bed because I got a Half Price Books gift card from Santa that I'm itching to spend.)

Posted January 4, 2013.

Bonnie ZoBell

Bonnie ZoBell's new linked collection from Press 53, *What Happened Here: a Novella and Stories*, is centered on the PSA Flight 182 crash into North Park, San Diego, in 1978, and features the imaginary characters who live there now. Her fiction chapbook *The Whack-Job Girls* was published in March 2013. She received a National Endowment for the Arts fellowship in fiction, the Capricorn Novel Award, and a PEN Syndicated Fiction Award. She received an MFA from Columbia University on fellowship, currently teaches at San Diego Mesa College, and is working on a novel.

Visit her website at bonniezobell.com, or read an excerpt from her latest at wewantedtobewriters.com/2014/02/excerpt-of-bonnie-zobells-new-book.

I have a conveyor-belt system moving books onto my bedside table. First, I place a bunch there. Slowly they manage to get read—or not read. Often I'm reading several at a time. Some have already been read. When the stack is exhausted, I put the read and the never-seemed-to-have-gotten-read into the trunk of my car, drive them to work and give them to my fiction-writing students. Then I put another stack on my bedside table, a stack that until now has been living somewhere else in the house, lying in wait on the dining room table, the kitchen counter, in a bookcase, or on the floor. Then I start over again.

At the moment, I have seven books and one magazine sitting by the bed.

Reading Now

Big Brother by **Lionel Shriver** — This is about a morbidly obese brother who's come to visit (read live) with his sister, her husband and their kids. It's difficult to decide whom to dislike more: the enormous brother who feels entitled to anything he wants, or his slightly overweight and very successful sister who orders him around. The psychology of Shriver's books is what I love about them. Such seemingly normal people with normal problems, but she goes in deep. Love her insight into sibling relationships, the love and the hate, the competition, and everything else that goes with the territory.

Recently Finished

Lionel Shriver, *We Need to Talk about Kevin* — I often like to read several books by the same author near each other in time to see what that writer is up to. This novel was every bit as well written and complex as the one I'm reading now and about a teenage boy who shoots up his high school. It was difficult to decide whom to dislike more: the violent ne'er-do-well son, or his icy mother. Fascinating to read how dislikable characters are handled by this author, who manages to get me to love her stories despite this. Love the insight into working mothers, women who don't want to have children, being a step-parent.

Roy Kesey, *Any Deadly Thing* — Astounding. I'd recently read and loved *Pacazo*, his most recent book and a novel, which had already gone onto my last student stack and was given to a student I knew would love it. This new book is very different than the novel, showing what a range Kesey has. The beauty of his language is awe-inspiring. The stories are set all over the world. How he seems to get right to the core of who we are and our moral struggles is remarkable.

Three Books I'm Savoring Bits of While Finishing Shriver's Novel

Cris Mazza, *Something Wrong with Her* — A "real-time memoir" that seems to defy categorization and on a subject that would make most other writers uncomfortable—anorgasmia or, to put it in old-fashioned terms, "frigidity." Mazza reads over her own past books to try to find the key to how this problem started, communicates with the man she feels contributed to starting it, as the two of them grapple with how it could have happened. Fascinating.

James Claffey, *Blood a Cold Blue* — Shows a mastery of language in very short stories, or poems, that often take us back to his native Dublin. The way he expresses grief and tragedy, the depth of feeling, is heartbreaking.

Heather Fowler, *This Time While We're Awake* — The mistress of the surreal. Beautiful tales in dystopian landscapes. The humor slays me, as does the wild imagination displayed in her plots, her fantastic yet very real characters, and the darkness seeping through.

Don't Tell My Students

People — Want to make something of it? Yes, I savor my *People* magazines after those days on which I've graded too many papers or not had enough sleep. This gives me the opportunity to not much care about anything but whether any of the Kardashians are getting divorced. From the beginning of time!

Posted May 2, 2014.

BOOKS BY OUR CONTRIBUTORS

Larry Baker

The Education of Nancy Adams (Ice Cube Press, 2014)

Love and Other Delusions (Ice Cube Press, 2013)

A Good Man (Ice Cube Press, 2009)

Athens/America (First Coast Books, 2005)

The Flamingo Rising (Knopf, 1997)

Nichole Bernier

The Unfinished Work of Elizabeth D. (Crown/Random House, 2012 & Broadway/Random House, 2013)

Miranda Beverly-Whittemore

Bittersweet (Crown Publishing, 2014)

Set Me Free (Warner Books, 2007)

The Effects of Light (Warner Books, 2005)

David Corbett

Save By An Evil Chance (Thomas & Mercer, forthcoming, April 2015)

The Art of Character (Penguin, January 2013)

The Devil's Redhead (MysteriousPress.com/Open Road, May 2012)

Done For a Dime (MysteriousPress.com/Open Road, May 2102)

Blood of Paradise (MysteriousPress.com/Open Road,

November 2012)

Do They Know I'm Running? (MysteriousPress.com/Open Road, November 2012)

Killing Yourself to Survive: Stories (MysteriousPress.com/Open Road, May 2012)

Matt Debenham

The Book of Right and Wrong (Ohio State University Press, 2010)

Julia Fierro

Cutting Teeth (St. Martin's Press, 2014)

Kathie Giorgio

Rise From The River (forthcoming)

Learning To Tell (A Life) Time (Main Street Rag Publishing Company, 2013)

Enlarged Hearts (Main Street Rag Publishing Company, 2012)

The Home For Wayward Clocks (Main Street Rag Publishing Company, 2011)

Erica Goss

Vibrant Words: Ideas and Inspirations for Poets (PushPen Press 2014)

Wild Place (Finishing Line Press 2012)

Sally Koslow

The Widow Waltz (Plume, 2014)

Slouching Toward Adulthood: How to Let Go So Your Kids Can Grow Up (Plume, 2013)

With Friends Like These (Ballantine Books, 2011)

The Late, Lamented Molly Marx (Ballantine Books, 2010)

Little Pink Slips (Berkley Trade, 2008)

Tom Molanphy

Loud Memories of a Quiet Life (Outpost 19, 2012)

Linda Rodriguez

Every Hidden Fear: a Skeet Bannion Mystery (Minotaur Books, 2014)

Every Broken Trust: A Skeet Bannion Mystery (Minotaur Books, 2013)

Every Last Secret: A Skeet Bannion Mystery (Minotaur Books, 2012)

Skin Hunger (Potpourri Publications, 1994; Scapegoat Press, 2007)

Heart's Migration (Tia Chucha Press, 2009)

Editor, *Woven Voices: 3 Generations of Puertorriqueña Poets Look at Their American Lives* (Scapegoat Press, 2013).

The "I Don't Know How To Cook" Book: Mexican (Adams Media, 2008)

James Schwartz

Arrival and Departure (Writing Knights Press, 2014)

The Literary Party: Growing Up Gay and Amish in America (InGroup Press, 2011)

Poetry in:
Arrival and Departure (Writing Knights Press, 2014); *Milk and Honey* (Siren, 2013); *Alpine Suite* (2013); *Poetry 4 Food 2* (2013); and *Among the Leaves: Queer Male Poets on the Midwestern Experience* (2012)

Dani Shapiro

Still Writing: The Pleasures and Perils of a Creative Life (Atlantic Monthly Press, 2013)

Devotion: A Memoir (Harper Perennial, 2011)

Slow Motion: A Memoir of a Life Rescued by Tragedy (Harper Perennial, 2010)

Black & White (Anchor Reprint, 2008)

Family History (Anchor Reprint, 2004)

Ann Elia Stewart

Twice a Child (Sunbury Press, 2012)

Susan Tepper

The Merrill Diaries (Pure Slush Books, 2013)

From the Umberplatzen (Wilderness House Press, 2012)

What May Have Been: Letters of Jackson Pollock & Dori G: A Novel, co-authored with Gary Percesepe (Cervena Barva Press, 2010)

Tom Titus — *Blackberries in July: A Forager's Field Guide to Inner Peace* (Red Moons Press, 2012)

Lee Upton

The Tao of Humiliation: Short Stories. (BOA Editions, 2014)

Swallowing the Sea: On Writing & Ambition, Boredom, Purity & Secrecy (Tupelo Press, 2012)

The Guide to the Flying Island (Miami University Press, 2009)

Undid in the Land of Undone (New Issues Press, 2007)

Suzy Vitello

The Moment Before (Diversion Books, 2014)

The Empress Chronicles (Diversion Books, 2014)

Unkiss Me: Stories (Freisinger Press, 2013)

Bonnie ZoBell

What Happened Here: A Novella and Stories (Press 53, 2014)

The Whack-Job Girls (Monkey Puzzle Press, 2013)

BOOKS DISCUSSED

FICTION

Including novels, short stories, drama, anthologies, young adult, and graphic novels

A

Jason Aaron and **R.M. Guéra**, *Scalped Volume 1: Indian Country* (Vertigo, 2007), pg 21

Diane Ackerman, *The Zookeeper's Wife* (W.W. Norton & Company, 2008), pg 39

Margaret Atwood, *MaddAddam* (Bloomsbury, 2013); *The Year of the Flood* (Anchor Reprint Edition, 2010); and *Oryx and Crake* (Anchor Reprint Edition, 2004), pg 32

Shalom Auslander *Hope: A Tragedy* (Riverhead Trade, 2012), pg 23

B

James Baldwin, *Another Country* (Vintage International, 1993), pg 74

Charles Baxter, *Believers* (Pantheon, 1997); and *The Feast of Love* (Vintage, 2001), pg 42

Stephen Beachy, *Boneyard* (Verse Chorus Press, 2011), pg 59

W.H. Beck, *Malcolm at Midnight* (Illustrated by Brian Lies, HMH Books for Young Readers, 2012), pg 18

Aimee Bender, *The Particular Sadness of Lemon Cake* (Random House, 2010), pg 70; and *Willful Creatures: Stories* (Anchor Reprint Edition, 2006), pg 88

David Benioff, *City of Thieves* (Plume, 2009), pg 21

Miranda Beverly-Whittemore, *Bittersweet* (Crown, 2014), pg 25

Robin Black, *Life Drawing* (Random House, 2014), pg 24

Amy Bloom, *Away* (Random House Trade Paperback, 2008), pg 21

Jenna Blum, *Those Who Save Us* (Houghton Mifflin Harcourt, Reprint, 2005), pg 39

Chris Bohjalian, *The Sandcastle Girls* (Vintage Contemporaries, 2013), pg 8

Charlotte Brontë, *Jane Eyre* (Michael O'Mara Reprint Edition, 2011), pg 53

Geraldine Brooks, *People of the Book* (Penguin Books, Reprint Edition, 2008); and *Year of Wonders: A Novel of the Plague* (Penguin Reprint Edition, 2002), pg 7

Ed Brubaker and **Sean Phillips**, *Sleeper Omnibus* (Vertigo, 2013); *Fatale, Book 1* (Image Comics, 2012); *Incognito* (Marvel, 2009); and *Criminal, Volumes 1-5* (Marvel, 2007-2010), pg 21

A.S. Byatt, *Possession* (Vintage, 1991), pg 11

C

Truman Capote, *A Capote Reader* (Penguin Books, 2002); and *The Grass Harp: Including A Tree of Night and Other Stories* (Vintage Reprint Edition, 1993), pg 60

Don Carpenter, *Hard Rain Falling* — with an introduction by George Pelecanos (New York Review Books Classics, 2009), pg 16

Joy Castro, *Nearer Home: a Nola Cespedes Mystery* (Thomas Dunne, 2013); and *Hell or High Water* (Thomas Dunne Books, 2012), pgs 36 & 55

Kelly Cherry, *A Kind of Dream: Stories* (University of Wisconsin Press, 2014), pg 29

James Claffey, *Blood a Cold Blue* (Press 53, 2013), pg 91

Suzanne Collins, *The Hunger Games* (Scholastic Press, 2010), pg 88

Julio Cortázar, *Blow-Up and Other Stories* (Pantheon, 1985), pg 80

Michael Cunningham, *Flesh and Blood* (Simon and Schuster, 1996); *The Hours* (Picador, 2000); and *Specimen Days* (Farrar, Straus & Giroux, 2005), pg 62

D

Lydia Davis, *Can't and Won't: Stories* (Farrar, Strauss & Giroux, 2014), pg 82

Despair, Inc., *Who Killed John F. Kennedy* (Despair, Inc., 2013), pg 69

Pete Dexter, *Spooner* (Grand Central Publishing, September 2009), pg 16

Anita Diamant, *The Red Tent* (Picador, 2007), pg 33

Keith Donohue, *The Boy Who Drew Monsters* (Picador, 2014); and *The Stolen Child* (Anchor Reprint Edition, 2007), pg 4

Erika Dreifus, *Quiet Americans* (Last Light Studio, 2011), pg 17

E

Anne Enright, *The Gathering* (Grove/Atlantic, 2007), pg 37

F

Hans Fallada, *Every Man Dies Alone* — translated by Michael Hofmann (Melville House, 2010), pg 40

Joshua Max Feldman, *The Book of Jonah* (Henry Holt & Co, 2014), pg 33

Jennie Fields, *The Age of Desire* (Viking Penguin, 2012), pgs 14 & 72

Jack Finney, *Time and Again* (Scribner Paperback Edition, 1995), pg 40

F. Scott Fitzgerald, *The Great Gatsby* (Scribner, Reissue Edition, 2004), pg 62 & 71

E.M. Forster, *Howard's End* (Dover Publications, 2002); and *Maurice* (W.W. Norton Reissue Edition, 2005), pg 51

Heather Fowler, *This Time While We're Awake* (Aqueous Books, 2013), pg 91

G

Mary Gaitskill, *Two Girls, Fat and Thin* (Simon & Schuster Reprint Edition, 1998), pg 88

Jane Gardam, *Crusoe's Daughter* (Europa Editions, 2012 paperback edition; originally published 1985), pg 53

William Gay, *I Hate To See That Evening Sun Go Down* (Free Press, 2003), pg 68

David Gillham, *City of Woman* (Berkley Trade, Reprint, 2013), pg 39

David Gilbert, *& Sons* (Random House, 2014), pg 64

Elizabeth Gilbert, *The Signature of All Things* (Penguin Books, 2014), pg 64

Robert Goolrick, *A Reliable Wife* (Algonquin Books, 2010), pg 17

Andrew Sean Greer, *The Story of a Marriage* (Picador, 2009), pg 88

David Grossman, *The End of the Land* (Vintage, Reprint Edition, 2011), pg 40

H

Chad Harbach, *The Art of Fielding* (Back Bay Books, Reprint edition, 2012), pg 8

Ursula Hegi, *Stones from the River* (Simon and Schuster, 1997), pg 33

Mark Helprin, *Memoir from Antproof Case* (Harcourt Brace, 1995), pg 74

Linda Hogan, *Mean Spirit* (Ivy Books, 1991), pg 57

Alan Hollinghurst, *The Stranger's Child* (Vintage, 2012 paperback edition); and *The Line of Beauty* (Bloomsbury, 2005), pg 51

A.M. Homes, *May We Be Forgiven* (Penguin Books, Reprint edition September, 2013), pg 15

Caroline Hwang, *In Full Bloom* (Penguin Books, 2003), pg 37

I

Bob Inman, *The Govenor's Lady* (John F. Blair, 2013); *Dairy Queen Days* (Amazon Digital Services, 2012); and *Captain Saturday* (Amazon Digital Services, 2012), pg 4

J

Shirley Jackson, *Shirley Jackson: Novels and Stories* — edited by Joyce Carol Oates (Library of America, 2010), pg 14

Mira Jacob, *The Sleepwalker's Guide to Dancing* (Random House, 2014), pg 25

Howard Jacobson, *The Finkler Question* (Bloomsbury USA, 2010), pg 39

Henry James, *Portrait of a Lady* (Penguin Classics, 2011), pg 39

P.D. James, *A Taste for Death* (Vintage Reprint Edition, 2005), pg 10

Victoria M. Johnson, *The Substitute Bride* (Kindle edition, 2012), pg 36

Antony Johnston, *Wasteland Book 1: Cities in Dust* (Oni Press, 2007), pg 21

Edward P. Jones, *All Aunt Hagar's Children* (Amistad, 2007); and *Lost in the City: Stories* (Amistad, 2003), pg 49

K

Sok-kyung Kang, **Chi-won Kim**, and **Chong-hui O**, *Words of Farewell: Stories by Korean Women Writers* (Seal Press, 1989), pg 37

Sayed Kashua, *Second Person Singular* — translated by Mitch Ginsburg (Grove Press, 2013), pg 40

Laura Kasischke, *Mind of Winter* (Harper, 2014), pg 29

Roy Kesey, *Any Deadly Thing* (Dzanc Books, 2013); and *Pacazo* (Dzanc Books, 2011), pg 90

L

Adam Langer, *Crossing California* (Riverhead, 2004), pg 42

John le Carré, *The Russia House* (Scribner Reprint Edition, 2004), pg 8

Don Lee, *The Collective* (W.W. Norton, 2012), pg 35

Dennis Lehane, *Sacred* (HarperCollins, 2010 paperback edition, originally published 1997), pg 52

Doris Lessing, *The Fifth Child* (Knopf, 1988), pg 43

Deborah Levy, *Swimming Home* (Bloomsbury USA, 2012), pg 20

Penelope Lively, *Moon Tiger* (Grove Press, 1997), pg 39

Margot Livesey, *The Flight of Gemma Hardy* (HarperCollins, 2012 Kindle edition), pg 53

Lorraine López, *The Realm of Hungry Spirits* (Grand Central Publishing, 2011); *Homicide Survivors Picnic* (BkMkPress, 2009); and *The Gifted Gabaldon Sisters* (Grand Central Publishing, 2008), pg 56

Lois Lowry, *Sons* — Book 4 in the *Giver Quartet* (HMH Books for Young Readers, Reissue Edition, 2014), pg 18

M

Patricia Ann McNair, *The Temple of Air: Stories* (Elephant Rock Productions, 2011), pg 17

Ian McEwan, *Atonement* (Anchor, 2003), pg 11

Claire Messud, *The Woman Upstairs* (Vintage Contemporaries, 2014), pg 38

Herman Melville, *Moby-Dick* (Dover Publications, 2003; first U.S. publication, Harper & Brothers, 1851), pg 23

David Mitchell, *Cloud Atlas* (Random House, 2004 paperback edition), pg 52

Nancy Mitford, *The Pursuit of Love* (Vintage, 2010), pg 39

Alan Moore and **Eddie Campbell** *From Hell* (Top Shelf Production, 2004), pg 21

Lorrie Moore, *Bark: Stories* (Knopf, 2014); pg 29

Susanna Moore, *The Life of Objects* (Vintage, 2013); pg 39

Grant Morrison, *The Invisibles*, Volume 1 (Vertigo, 2013); pg 21

Iris Murdoch, *The Sea, The Sea* (Penguin, 2008); pgs 39 & 81

N

Vladimir Nabokov, *Lolita* (Vintage Reissue, 1989); pg 39

O

Joyce Carol Oates, *Them* (Modern Library Reprint Edition, 2006); pg 87

Flannery O'Conner, *A Good Man Is Hard To Find* (Harcourt Brace Jovanovich, 1977), pg 45; and *Complete Stories*, (originally published 1971 by Farrar, Straus and Giroux), pgs 47 & 85

Mary Pope Osborne, *The Magic Treehouse* series (Random House Books for Young Readers, 2001), pg 26

P

Christopher Paolini, *Inheritance Cycle* (Knopf Books for Young Readers, 2012), pg 19

David Plante, *The Age of Terror* (St. Martin's Press, 2000), pg 8

R

Marilynne Robinson, *Gilead* (Picador Reprint, 2006), pgs 39 & 68

Linda Rodriguez, *Every Last Secret* (St. Martin's, 2012), pg 36

Salman Rushdie, *Midnight's Children* (Jonathan Cape, 1980), pg 23

Karen Russell, *Swamplandia!* (Alfred A. Knopf, 2011), pg 36

Hank Phillippi Ryan, *The Wrong Girl* (Forge Books, 2013); and *The Other Woman* (Forge Books, Reissue, 2013), pg 57

S

Maria Semple, *This One is Mine* (Little, Brown & Co., 2008); and *Where'd You Go, Bernadette* (Back Bay Books, Reprint Edition, 2013), pg 41

George Bernard Shaw, *Back to Methuselah* (Dodd, Mead & Company, 1963), pg 13

Lionel Shriver, *Big Brother* (Harper Perennial, Reprint Edition, 2014), pg 89; and *We Need to Talk About Kevin* (Harper Perennial, 2006), pg 90

Leslie Marmon Silko, *Ceremony* — with an introduction by Larry McMurtry (Penguin Books, Anniversary Edition, 2006), pg 18

Shelter Somerset, *Between Two Worlds* (Dreamspinner Press, 2011); *Between Two Promises* (Dreamspinner Press, 2011); and *Between Two Loves* (Dreamspinner Press, 2013), all part of the *Between Two Worlds* series, pg 59

Tom Spanbauer, *I Loved You More* (April, 2014, Hawthorne Books), pg 83

Julia Spencer-Fleming, *Through the Evil Days* (Minotaur Books, 2013); and *One Was a Soldier* (Minotaur Books, 2012), pg 56

Muriel Spark, *The Girls of Slender Means* (New Directions, 1998), pg 39

Edward St. Aubyn, *The Patrick Melrose Novels: Never Mind, Bad News, Some Hope,* and *Mother's Milk* (Picador, 2012), pgs 39 & 82

Wallace Stegner, *Crossing to Safety* (Modern Library Classics, 2002); and *Angle of Repose* (Penguin Classics, 2000), pg 8

William Styron, *Darkness Visible* (Random House, 1990), pg 37

Duane Swierczynski, *The Blonde* (St. Martin's Griffin, 2007), pg 15

T

J.R.R. Tolkien, *The Fellowship of the Ring* (Mariner Books Reissue, 2012), pg 53

William Trevor, *The Collected Stories* (Penguin Books, 1992), pg 74

Anne Tyler, *The Accidental Tourist* (A Berkley Book/ Alfred Knopf, 1985), pg 71

V

Jeff Vandermeer, *Annihilation* — from the *Southern Reach Trilogy* (Farrar, Straus & Giroux Originals, 2014), pg 25

Brian K. Vaughan and **Pia Guerra**, *Y: The Last Man, Book 1* (Vertigo, 2008), pg 21

W

Ayelet Waldman, *Love and Other Impossible Pursuits* (Doubleday, 2006), pg 43

Jess Walter, *Beautiful Ruins* (Harper Perennial Reprint, 2013), pg 84

Sarah Waters, *Fingersmith* (Virago Press, 2002), pg 72

Jincy Willett, *Amy Falls Down* (Thomas Dunne Books, 2013); and *Winner of the National Book Award: A Novel of Fame, Honor, and Really Bad Weather* (Picador, 2004), pg 5

Virginia Woolf, *To The Lighthouse* (Harcourt Brace Jovanovich, 1989), pg 11

Meg Wolitzer, *The Interestings* (Riverhead, 2014), pg 64

Martha Woodroof, *Small Blessings* (St. Martin's Press, 2014), pg 5

Z

Markus Zusak, *The Book Thief* (Alfred A. Knopf, 2007), pg 40

POETRY

Including translations and anthologies

A

A.R. Ammons, editor, *Best American Poetry 1994* (Simon & Schuster, 1994), pg 37

Catherine Anderson, *Woman with a Gambling Mania* (Mayapple Press, 2014), pg 56

Allison Adelle Hedge Coke, editor, *SING: Poetry from the Indigenous Americas* (University of Arizona Press, 2011); *Blood Run* (Salt Publishing, 2007); and *Dog Road Woman* (Coffee House Press, 1998), pg 55

Hart Crane, *The Bridge* (Fordham University Press, Annotated Edition, 2011), pg 61

D

John Daniel, *Of Earth* (Lost Horse Press, 2012), pg 78

E

Susan Elbe, *The Map of What Happened* (Backwaters Press, 2013), pg 30

G

Max Garland, *Postal Confessions* (University of Massachusetts Press, 1995), pg 30

H

Brooks Haxton, translator, *Dances for Flute and Thunder: Praises, Prayers, and Insults, Poems from The Ancient Greek* (Viking Press, 1999), pg 62

Linda Hogan, *Rounding the Human Corners* — with an introduction by William Kittredge (Coffee House Press, 2008), pg 57

K

Julia Spicher Kasdorf, *Sleeping Preacher* (Pitt Poetry Series, University of Pittsburgh Press, 1992), pg 59

P

Simon Perchik, *Hands Collected: The Books of Simon Perchik* (Pavement Saw Press, 2000); and *Almost Rain* (River Otter Press, 2013), pg 73

R

Adrienne Rich, *Tonight No Poetry Will Serve: Poems 2007-2010* (W.W. Norton, 2011), pg 34

Kathryn Ridall, editor, *What the River Brings: Oregon River Poems: River Poems by 56 Oregon Poets* (Fae Press, 2011), pg 78

Arthur Rimbaud, *Illuminations* — translated by John Ashbery (W.W. Norton, 2012), pg 61

Robin Robertson, *Slow Air* (Picador, 2002), pg 82

Levi Romero, *A Poetry of Remembrance: New and Rejected Works* (University of New Mexico Press, 2009), pg 58

S

Publius Papinius Statius, *The Thebaid: Seven Against Thebes* — translated by Charles Stanley Ross (Johns Hopkins University Press, 2007), pg 50

Frank Stanford, *The Battlefield Where The Moon Says I Love You* (Lost Roads Publishers, 2000), pg 69

T

Natasha Threthewey, *Native Guard* (Houghton Mifflin, 2006), pg 36

Tomas Transtromer, *The Great Enigma* — translated by Robin Fulton (New Directions, 2006), pg 61

V

Paul Verlaine, *Paul Verlaine: Selected Poems* (Oxford University Press, 2009), pg 61

W

Walt Whitman, *Leaves of Grass* (Library of America, 1982), pg 57

Tim Whitsel, *We Say Ourselves* (Traprock Books, 2014), pg 78

Charles Wright, *Bye-and-Bye: Selected Late Poems* (Farrar, Straus & Giroux, 2011), pg 69

NONFICTION

Including histories, biographies, essays, memoirs, and anthologies

A

Rick Atkinson, *The Day of Battle: The War In Sicily and Italy, 1943-44* (Volume Two of the Liberation Trilogy) (Holt Paperbacks, 2008), pg 26

B

Richard Beeman, *Plain Honest Men: The Making of the American Constitution* (Random House, 2010), pg 3

Sylvia Boorstein, *Happiness is an Inside Job* (Ballantine, 2008), pg 63

Cleanth Brooks and **Robert Penn Warren**, *Understanding Poetry* (Holt, Rinehart and Winston, 4th editon, 1976), pg 50

Brené Brown, *Daring Greatly: How the Courage to Be Vulnerable Transforms the Way We Live, Love, Parent, and Lead* (Gothan, 2012), pg 86

Jean de La Bruyère, *Characters* (Penguin Classics, January 1970), pg 15

Janet Burroway, editor, *A Story Larger Than My Own: Women Writers Look Back on Their Lives and Careers* (University of Chicago, 2014), pg 82

C

Joseph Campbell, *Hero With a Thousand Faces* (New World Library, 2008), pg 22

Mary Cantwell, *Manhattan Memoir* (Penguin Books, 2000), pg 65

Truman Capote, *In Cold Blood* (Vintage, 1994), pg 60

Joy Castro, *Island of Bones: Essays* (University of Nebraska Press, 2012), pgs 36 & 55; and *The Truth Book: a Memoir* (University of Nebraska Press, 2012), pg 55

Gary Chapman, *The 5 Love Languages* (Moody Publishers/Northfield Publishing, 1992), pg 71

Allison Adelle Hedge Coke, *Rock, Ghost, Willow, Deer: A Story of Survival* (Bison Books, Reprint Edition, 2014), pg 55

Trevor Corson, *The Secret Life of Lobsters* (HarperCollins, 2005 paperback edition; originally published 2004), pg 52

D

Dalai Lama, aka **Lhamo Dondrub**, aka **Tenzin Gyatso**, *The Art of Happiness* (Riverhead, 10th Anniversary Edition, 2009), pg 9

John Daniel, *Rogue River Journal* (Counterpoint, 2005); and *Winter Creek: One Writer's Natural History* (Milkweed Editions, 2002), pg 75

Joan Didion, *Slouching Towards Bethlehem* (Farrar, Straus & Giroux, 1961), pg 35

Annie Dillard, *The Writing Life* (Harper Perennial, 2013), pg 64

E

David Eagleman, *Sum: Forty Tales from the Afterlives* (Vintage, 2010), pg 64

Gretel Ehrlich, *The Solace of Open Spaces* (Penguin Books, 1986), pg 47

G

Diane Glancy, *Claiming Breath* (Bison Books, 1996), pg 58

H

Janet Campbell Hale, *Bloodlines: Odyssey of a Native Daughter* (University of Arizona Press, 1997), pg 18

Clinton Heylin, *From the Velvets to the Voidoids: The Birth of American Punk Rock* (Chicago Review Press, 2005), pg 22

Zora Neale Hurston, *Dust Tracks on a Road* (Harper Perennial, 1942), pg 69

J

Marilyn Johnson, *The Dead Beat: Lost Souls, Lucky Stiffs, and the Perverse Pleasures of Obituaries* (Harper Collins, 2006), pg 66

K

Nicole C. Kear, *Now I See You* (St. Martin's Press, 2014), pg 11

Robin Wall Kimmerer, *Braiding Sweetgrass: Indigenous Wisdom, Scientific Knowledge and the Teachings of Plants* (Milkweed Editions, 2013); and *Gathering Moss: a Natural and Cultural History of Mosses* (Oregon State University Press, 2003), pg 77

Jack Kornfield, *After the Ecstasy, the Laundry* (Bantam, 2001), pg 9; and *A Path With Heart: A Guide Through the Perils and Promises of Spiritual Life* (Bantam, 1993), pg 63

L

Anne Lamott, *Bird by Bird: Some Instructions on Writing and Life* (Anchor, 1995), pg 87

Mark Larrimore, editor, *The Problem of Evil: A Reader* (Wiley-Blackwell, 2000), pg 16

Aldo Leopold, *A Sand County Almanac* (Ballantine Books, 1986), pg 76

Jerome Loving, *Walt Whitman: The Song of Himself* (University of California Press, 1999), pg 74

M

D.T. Max, *Every Love Story is a Ghost Story: A Life of David Foster Wallace* (Viking Adult, 2012), pg 43

Cris Mazza, *Something Wrong with Her* (Jaded Ibis Press, 2013), pg 90

Robert McKee, *Story: Style, Structure, Substance, and the Principles of Screenwriting* (Harper Collins e-books, 2010), pg 22

John McPhee, *Assembling California* (Farrar, Straus & Giroux, 1994), pg 46

Rebecca Mead, *My Life in Middlemarch* (Crown, 2014), pg 80

Reid J. Meloy, *The Psychopathic Mind: Origins, Dynamics, and Treatment* (Jason Aronson, Inc., 1988), pg 16

Deborah Miranda, *Bad Indians: A Tribal Memoir* (Heyday, 2013), pg 55

N

Kathleen Norris, *Dakota: A Spiritual Geography* (Mariner, 2001), pg 32

O

Flannery O'Conner, *The Habit of Being: Letters of Flannery O'Connor*, selected and edited by Sally Fitzgerald (Farrar, Straus & Giroux, 1979), pg 69

George Orwell, *Down and Out in Paris and London* (Houghton Mifflin Harcourt, 1972); *Burmese Days* (Houghton Mifflin Harcourt, 1974); and *Fifty Essays* (Benediction Classics, 2010), pg 13

P

Robert Michael Pyle, *The Tangled Bank* (Oregon State University Press, 2012), pg 77

R

David Rakoff, *Half Empty* (Doubleday, 2010), pg 87

Katherine Ramsland, *The Criminal Mind* (Writers Digest Books, 2002), pg 16

Nick Reding, *Methland: The Death and Life of an American Small Town* (Bloomsbury, 2009), pg 16

S

Mark Salzman, *True Notebooks: A Writer's Year at Juvenile Hall* (Vintage, 2004), pg 44

George Schenk, *Moss Gardening: Including Lichens, Liverworts, and Other Miniatures* (Timber Press, 1997), pg 81

Stacy Schiff, *Cleopatra: A Life* (Little, Brown and Company/Hachette Book Group, 2010), pg 71

Stendahl, aka Marie-Henri Beyle, *De l'amour* (BiblioLife, 2009), pg 15

Martha Stout, *The Sociopath Next Door* (Harmony, 2006), pg 16

Cheryl Strayed, *Tiny Beautiful Things* (Vintage, 2012), pg 86

T

Edward Teller and **Judith Shoolery**, *Memoirs: A Twentieth-Century Journey in Science and Politics* (Perseus Publishing, 2001), pg 14

Theophrastus, *Moral Character* — translated by Eustace Budgell (Ulan Press, 2011), pg 15

Abigail Thomas, *A Three Dog Life* (Harcourt, Inc., 2006), pg 67

Tomas Transtromer, *Memories Look at Me: A Memoir* — translated by Robin Fulton (New Directions, 2011), pg 61

Mark Twain, *Life on the Mississippi* (Project Gutenberg ebook), pg 13

V

Christopher Vogler, *The Writer's Journey: Mythic Structure for Wrtiers, 3rd Edition* (Michael Wiese Productions, 2007), pg 21

Patricia Volk, *Stuffed: Adventures of a Restaurant Family* (Vintage, 2002); and *Shocked: My Mother, Schiaparelli, and Me* (Knopf, 2013), pg 40

Y

Kevin Young, *The Grey Album: On The Blackness of Blackness* (Greywolf Press, 2012), pg 69

Neil Young, *Waging Heavy Peace* (Blue Rider Press, Penguin Group, 2012), pg 66

Lidia Yuknavitch, *The Chronology of Water* (Hawthorne Books & Literary Arts, 2010), pg 36

Z

Connie Zweig and **Jeremiah Abrams**, editors, *Meeting the Shadow: The Hidden Power of the Dark Side of Human Nature* (Tarcher, 1991), pg 16

ABOUT THE EDITORS

The members of Team Olsen have long since overcome the feeling that the other was hogging all the creative molecules in the house and exerting undue pressure on noisy keyboards. After four-plus decades of wordmongering, Cheryl and Eric happily maintain separate home offices, literary tastes, and styles. The husband and wife writers edit each other's written work—and sometimes spoken language as well. Every once in awhile, they put aside their respective creative endeavors to work on a project together that renews their faith in the transformative power of words. This book is one of those projects.

www.ingramcontent.com/pod-product-compliance
Lightning Source LLC
Chambersburg PA
CBHW071928130726
47909CB00014B/2638